THE PERFECT PRESIDENT

THE PERFECT PRESIDENT

A Novel

Mark Moorstein

Author of Red Reflections and Frameworks:
Conflict in Balance

iUniverse, Inc.
New York Lincoln Shanghai

THE PERFECT PRESIDENT

iUniverse books may be ordered through booksellers or by contacting:

iUniverse
2021 Pine Lake Road, Suite 100
Lincoln, NE 68512
www.iuniverse.com
1-800-Authors (1-800-288-4677)

ISBN-13: 978-0-595-40609-8 (pbk)
ISBN-13: 978-0-595-84975-8 (ebk)
ISBN-10: 0-595-40609-2 (pbk)
ISBN-10: 0-595-84975-X (ebk)

Printed in the United States of America

To Muriel, Babs, Mac, Pavel, Ron, and Betty

Acknowledgments

The idea for this book began in the late 1990s when, for a project, I photographed the homeless in Washington, DC. The book took on greater life when I realized that the language of our government differed little from the language of the streets. Finally, I began to write last year in Rio de Janeiro when I ran into witty and clever homeless surviving on the beaches by dumping dog-droppings on tourist shoes and then offering shoe shines. I later discovered some of them sleeping on tree limbs outside my hotel.

I want to thank everyone that helped with the book, including family and friends who read the progressive manuscripts in exchange for lunches and dinners. I also want to thank my dogs, Beauregard and Hanna, who really would bite the leg off Santa Claus if he kicked me.

September 25, 2006

I

The kick not only shook me awake; it incensed Buster Keaton enough to chew the leg off of Santa Claus.

There in snow lit by the steam-diffused streetlights on a black-and-white Constitution Avenue, doing the hokey-pokey with my usually gentle mutt, was Saint Nick doling out blankets, baloney sandwiches, and black coffee that tasted like Potomac sewage when I finally got around to drinking it. I had fought hard for the heating grate and a few hours of sleep—and I sure as hell didn't feel like fighting again—especially with some red-suited dude dancing on the sidewalk with my dog. I had defended enough of my teeth for one night—especially during Christmas when I needed my jaw to wheedle money from tourists and do-gooders to survive until spring. Like all the hack politicos in Washington, DC, I just wanted to doze off to the hum of acrid hot air.

"Smitty!" Leroy shouted. "Grab his shit before the bitch boogies off with his reindeer."

I had forgotten that Leroy was sharing the grate with Buster Keaton and me beneath the monochrome mess that typified the treasures of the unchosen homeless. Leroy was big, bold, and black, bedecked in an army field jacket covered with snow that matched his white goatee. I was white and even bigger—and nearly twenty years younger—but we still needed to watch each other's frozen backsides when Santa Claus or anyone else came sliding down the street. We already had defended the grate from squatters after soliciting sightseers in town for the red, white, and green scenery on the south side of the White House.

"Thanks, man," Leroy said as he detached Buster Keaton's canines from Santa's shin. "Can you leave more of this stuff for my friends?"

Santa rubbed his leg. "My instructions are to give one blanket, one sandwich, and one cup of coffee to one person."

"What's this one man, one vote bullshit?" I grumbled. "Who gives Kris Kringle instructions? Mrs. Kringle? Dorothy on Kansas Avenue?"

"Where are your friends?" the fat man asked Leroy.

"Up in Lafayette Park—on the dark side of the White House where the trees don't twinkle."

"I'm going up there in a little while. Merry Christmas!"

"Ho ho ho, you motherfucker!"

II

OK, everyone knows you can fool some of the people all of the time, and all of the people some of the time, but you can't fool all of the people all of the time. And everyone believes Abraham Lincoln said it. But I think P. T. Barnum actually cooked up the quote as a remorseful response to his other line about a sucker being born every minute. I like Lincoln more than Barnum because Lincoln was tall like me and he told the truth—even if he manufactured mustier mutterings like, "He who molds public sentiment goes deeper than he who enacts statutes or pronounces decisions." But as I interpret both Honest Abe and P. T. Barnum, the Wizards of Oz of the world have more influence than Congress or the Supreme Court.

Everyone thinks George W. Bush—who was no Abraham F. Lincoln—won the presidential election in November 2000 and served two terms. But Bush didn't win—he didn't even wring the nomination from the Republicans. The winner was James Jefferson Jones, or J3, and he became the "Perfect President." He was, in my humble opinion, far better than Bush and even more perfect than Lincoln. How J3 accomplished his ascent and molded the musty American sentiment—how he fooled all of the people all of the time as a modern Wizard of Oz—should be told by me, one of the architects of his victory and term in office.

What makes this incredible, of course, is that history books, television, and the Internet of the year 2020, lacking twenty-twenty hindsight, say nothing about J3, his election, or his service to the nation. The whole world suffered amnesia—and skipped J3's part in history. "How is this possible?" you might ask.

First, let's talk about J3—especially because, despite what some would describe as nothing but wizardry, he *was* the Perfect President: responsive to the republic, nimble to nuances, willing to work with Congress and the

Supreme Court, proficient in foreign policy, a moral manager, handsome, athletic, brave, smart, creative, etc. etc. etc.

J3 was flawless—except for outbreaks of Tourette's syndrome, an uncontrollable sexual urge, and some other minor defects. As a child, he surely listened to his mother, cleaned his plate, and took naps faithfully. He went to the best schools, captained every sport, and won competitions that didn't depend on those who weren't as perfect as he was. He was gracious and complimentary in his victories—and everyone forgave his general flawlessness. He became the superlative scholar-athlete, majored in politics, and wrote an award-winning work about Anglo-American, anti-communist attitudes in Algeria. He graduated at the top of his class, won a Rhodes scholarship, and studied at Oxford. There, to the praise of his professors, he examined English nuts and colonial bolt production from 1721 to 1756.

This sort of *über*achievement by a WASP perfectionist kept up throughout his career, although—to be honest—it trapped him. J3 couldn't face anything without completing it faultlessly, which meant he remained too long in places. Although overstaying wasn't a good thing at parties, everyone admired his dedication and endowments after the parties.

Especially women. Being perfect can be perfectly boring, but J3 apparently did well in the sack. According to a class action lawsuit brought at the end of his term in office, J3 was handsome, high-strung, and well hung—and he tried out thousands of women. In the end, he never legally abandoned his wife, Linda—who, while not flawless, certainly was good looking, smart, and dignified.

As a person in charge, he pulled together people possessing less power. What choice did he have? To acquire mortals who met standards anywhere near his, J3 had to mine the planet, or he had to close his eyes and draw in pretenders. This is almost where I come in—but not quite. I was one of the unchosen pretenders who gravitated to the center of his world. My name is Jason Ward Smith IV (a name I put together in the pursuit of the White House)—or simply Smitty.

Here are *my* imperfections: I grew up parentless in the northeast part of DC, and I graduated only from elementary school. I grew tall and strong and fairly handsome for a white boy in a black city. People never picked on me because I pounded them into the pavement if they did. A few teachers tried to train me. Still, I couldn't follow rules. I gleaned whatever my hands grabbed—from the ancient Greeks to the modern geeks. But if I liked books, I didn't process ideas in any normal way. I'm sure I was missing a few wires—or maybe the electrons escaped from the circuits I did have. If a physics teacher explained how energy converted into matter, I calculated the energy to make an explanation matter. If someone taught that man evolved because he adapted to the environment, I evolved by manipulating the environment.

I never cared for politics; I sure as hell couldn't name half the presidents. I didn't worry much about money—except to survive. I didn't seek personal success, but I imagined new ways to do old things. And in thinking and doing things by myself I made mistakes that cost me friends, lovers, jobs—you name it. My chief characteristic obviously wasn't consistency, although I could show up anywhere on time. My greatest strength rested in my ability to adjust. If system X didn't work, I'd find system Y—or create it. Living beyond the limits made me charismatic, but no one could stomach charisma forever.

The result of all of this was inevitable. I became a homeless person on the streets of DC—usually downtown, but sometimes on Kansas Avenue, a long diagonal thoroughfare that cuts through the city, filled with neat townhouses, apartments, and parks where I knew people and found a safe haven. It all occurred gradually—spending the night sauntering up and down the streets, not paying the rent for my tiny apartment, then getting kicked out by an angry landlord, bumming food. It was an adventure in most respects because I had no responsibilities except to search for something to eat every day and someplace to sleep every night. I had complete freedom—even when my personal security remained at risk.

Lots of homeless folks lived on the streets and shelters of DC: women—sometimes with children—whose husbands had run off, unfortunates that fell through the so-called safety nets. Some were crazy. Still others just made bad decisions. I knew how to avoid precarious areas of DC and I made friends easily. We had an interesting, if not great community—and we long-term homeless watched out for each other. "Long-term homeless" was an oxymoron—because the homeless got sick and died, were institutionalized, went to jail—or some random event saved them before too much time passed. I wasn't crazy and I did earn a little money panhandling or making jewelry and selling it in Adams Morgan or in Lafayette Park. This little money allowed me to rent a locker and pay for things I needed. I wasn't completely unstructured. No one did anything to me except toss me in jail occasionally for drinking, fighting, or stealing. I never did drugs—drugs meant instant death. And I never slept with any woman without protection. That too meant instant death—or a slow, agonizing one, which was worse.

My best friend on the streets, a black man named Leroy Stivers, a proud Vietnam War hero, had worked as a DC cop, a city garbage collector, and a taxi driver. He even had a few grown kids and a daughter on the DC City Council. But he just couldn't keep it all together. Bill collectors and bankruptcy drove him out, and his children didn't appreciate his drinking. I once asked Leroy why he didn't control his alcoholism and live with his daughter, who cared about him. He told me she wouldn't let him watch TV after ten o'clock.

All of the homeless told stories, and they usually included long chapters of hard drinking, drugs, mental debilitation, violence, financial disaster, the inability to get along with people, or a compulsive desire to be alone. The homeless required an entire social department to sort out their dramas.

The government did help us in the cold winters that stripped the hues off the trees and gardens around DC. Most of the official buildings along Constitution Avenue—pale platforms that posted the mind-numbing practices inside—were centrally heated with steam. Heating grates rippled from the buildings, and each grate belonged to someone—or even a few people. Some of the homeless died fighting over them, but fighting seemed unnecessary because the government and charities provided shelters. Sometimes I slept on the grates to enjoy staring at the sky—but I liked the rank indoor beds better than suffering in the cold, even if I had trouble finding one that fit my long frame.

In the summer I hitchhiked to the beach towns—usually Ocean City—and crashed wherever I could. I worked occasionally at seasonal restaurants or on the beach at T-shirt and souvenir stores, but more often I just hung out on the boardwalks selling my stuff or simply loving the free life. Sometimes I rented a room for a day, slept in a real bed, shaved and then cleaned up to the point that I looked like a normal thirty-year-old. In the sun—especially on the beach—I looked even larger than my six feet, four inches and 210 pounds because I flexed my muscles and walked that howdy-stranger Texan walk George W. Bush perfected. I needed to look big to protect myself and the friends I trusted.

In the summer of 1998 I met Sarah Rivers on the OC boardwalk. She was out strolling in her bikini with her husband Paul and stopped to look at my jewelry. She had long brown hair, big blue eyes, a wide pretty smile, and one unbelievable body. She asked about the jewelry, and I told her I'd made most of it—but I'd bought some, found some, and even stolen some. She laughed at the honesty of my dishonesty. She could have purchased the same stuff at other places on the boardwalk; scam wholesalers covered the town with offers of commissions and consignments. These wholesalers ripped us off, but we ripped them off as well. I never paid for anything unless I had to. I almost never used violence to get something—and was against it in general—but I wasn't above taking something or conning the wholesalers if they couldn't play the game as well as I could.

Sarah bought the jewelry I made and told me I had talent. When she saw the showy seashells I sold by the seashore, she smirked. I think she just felt compassion because she was a do-gooder. I learned from her easy conversation, however, that she liked Ronald Reagan and that deep-red Republican blood ran through her veins. In any case, she was one beautiful woman with her own Bohemian streak. Despite that streak and her playfulness when I told her how hot she was, she seemed to approach life more seriously than I ever could.

Sarah had money—she drove a Mercedes—and an important job as a consultant in Washington. She told me that she and Paul, a lawyer who wore black socks with his tennis shoes and madras shorts, owned a few weeks of a timeshare in a highrise overlooking the beach. Paul grew impatient standing there while Sarah revealed everything—and told no one in particular that he hated to overheat his vital organs in the sun. Sarah ignored him while she prattled on about my "artwork" and the importance of creativity in the world.

Sarah stopped by every day of her vacation—at first she brought me ice cream or french fries. But eventually she just gave me money. She asked how I lived and I pretty much lied about my real condition. I told her I'd rented a small room for the summer with friends, but she could tell by my evasions that I didn't stay with anyone. She had an intuitive sense about my true nature and somehow knew I was rootless if not ruthless.

One day, out of the deep blue sky that enveloped OC and the sea, Sarah invited me into her timeshare for a week because she and Paul had to return early to Washington. "We have nearly two weeks left, and it doesn't make sense to let it go to waste—especially if you need a place to stay. We'll probably be back next weekend."

So I moved in and enjoyed a week of living well—not trashing the apartment as some of the homeless might if given a chance—until Sarah turned up again. Paul had left on a business trip to Brazil or Australia or someplace. I offered to move out—I wasn't predatory—but she insisted I stay.

For my part, I behaved myself. She was seductive in her business clothes—in fact, she was downright disarming dressed in anything more than her bikini. I understood that jumping on a woman could jet me to jail for the rest of my life. Fortunately, my restraint gave her confidence.

She certainly didn't need my attention—she already possessed poise and confidence to establish a successful career. She had a few years on me, but they made it easier to take orders—even if she confused me. She once asked me to connect her computer to a DSL line, but I had no idea how to flip on the switch, let alone connect some plug to the Internet. I made phone calls and read manuals and eventually figured it out, but I had no talent for technology. Sarah told me more than once that she liked me because I "deviated" from the Washington crowd. "Smitty, you remind me of no one. You're a clean slate." I wasn't sure what that meant—but she had plans. I enjoyed pleasing her because it was an easy bargain: all I had to do was obey her, and she gave me a free room.

And a few other things.

Sparks lit up every discussion, every evening stroll on the boardwalk, every meal, every swim, every goodnight and good morning. She wore one tiny bikini that blew me up faster than a boardwalk balloon. One morning before she left for the beach she asked me to rub sunscreen over her naked back, and this turned into a sunscreen massage of her front. Before long we were rubbing more than sunscreen.

Our sex was amazing—and she liked everything. We soon were connecting five or six times a day.

This kept up until a telephone call abruptly forced her to return to Washington. She ordered me out of the apartment—and except for a cold and a memory, I kept nothing of her.

III

Getting tossed out on my ass was a life lesson I understood without instruction: in order to regain the dubious freedom of the streets I had to surrender the security of a clean bed and good food. The two weeks at Sarah's—sleeping with her, eating regularly, and pretty much enjoying life—kindled a wish for a normal existence. It was, after all, easier to sit up and beg than growl. Needless to say, I found it hard to return to the streets.

Leroy, who had hitchhiked to OC to find his own work, sympathized with my waning enthusiasm for street life. When I told him about Sarah, he saw that I'd sold my wretched soul to her. "Avoid voodoo," he advised.

Despite my setback, I readapted to street life. I returned to selling my jewelry; but, post-Sarah, conning people as a great artist proved more difficult. No one wanted necklaces shaped from hot dog wrappers. I found a job in an arcade. I had to invite an endless stream of suckers to throw basketballs at undersized hoops. The work taught me that if you gave people something—a stuffed animal or the littlest bit of respect and admiration—they didn't care if you lied or stole their money. People preferred the joy of illusions to the hardship of reality.

One day a crew-cut teenager bounced into the arcade looking for a stuffed animal for the girlfriend attached to his bulging arm. I calculated that I could take all of his money if I let him show off a little. I goaded him into tossing the basketball again and again, but he never made a shot. I collected enough of his money to pay for ten stuffed animals—but after a while I identified with his embarrassment and offered him a free turn. I told him to shoot from another spot, the only place the rigged hoop would let the ball pass. He finally hit two in a row and broke into a grin. I gave him back his money along with a big stuffed dog. For this little bit of humanity, the manager fired me.

I'm sure the kid thought he achieved something as he walked out proudly. And I'm sure the arcade manager believed I'd embezzled money. Maybe someone thought I showed too much compassion for the dumb son-of-a-bitch. I'd known from filling out police reports that what really happened didn't matter. If you controlled the information seeping into an official head, you could make the innocent look guilty and the biggest criminal look like Mother Theresa. You could open or close any mind by feeding them bogus facts or limiting their vision. I once was shuffling down Kansas Avenue when some guy who'd shot a druggie on Georgia Avenue ran past me. I swore the guy was dressed in white but I'd focused on his gun—a shiny .38 Smith and Wesson that gangsters liked. The police chasing him asked if I'd seen anyone, and I described the man in white. They caught the guy, but it turned out he wore black. Somehow my mind switched things because I focused on the gun and not the clothes.

OC was far more peaceful and easy than Kansas and Georgia Avenues. Still, after losing my job at the arcade, I lived hand to mouth on the boardwalk with Leroy. I sometimes suggested new prospects to Leroy—such as selling advertising space on girls—but we needed capital, available girls, and a serious creative push to pull us out of our slump. "Why do we have to work so hard?" I asked.

"Because someone has to be the unchosen."

As the unchosen, we evolved our own strategies for survival. Even Freud recognized that the lowest species had a life force. Sure, we liked drinking, partying, sex, and irresponsibility—but we matched the chosen in that regard. Where rich folks drew their energy from money and the safety it bought, we drew it from the rhythms of the street. If you adapted to the street, you didn't need a clock, a cell phone, or an expectation. You lived from sunup to sundown, and then you followed the beat again and again until you died. Leroy thought getting off the street was like getting off the earth. "You know you'll just fall back." But I knew success required a strong will and a lot of risk-taking.

When the summer ended, Leroy and I hitchhiked back to DC and Kansas Avenue, the parks, the shelters, and the heating grates. Leroy liked Lafayette Park across the street from the White House, but I preferred to move around. Sometimes I stayed in a shelter near Capitol Hill with my friends Pigpen and Shark—who played poker better than anyone—and sometimes I stayed outdoors with Leroy and Carlos Rodriguez, a short Puerto Rican who wore earmuffs in the summer and couldn't smell anything except bad food. It all depended on the weather and events and the opportunity to take someone's money or pizza and beer. If crowds came to town, I slept on the grates because tourists paid me for the slightest trick. I could beg, borrow, or steal more in one big weekend than a month of normal days. Leroy, Carlos, and I staked out traffic intersections to shake down arriving sightseers.

Once I painted a big sign in shaky, childlike writing that said, "Will work for dog food. BK is hungry." This was true—although Buster Keaton, a young mutt that grew attached to me, belonged to everyone and no one. He roamed the streets distinguishing friend and foe more accurately than NORAD, but he attracted kids with his empathetic eyes. About one out of four cars gave us something—more often when Buster Keaton stared at the drivers—and in an hour we each made thirty or forty dollars. More than a few tourists seemed outraged that we had to survive this way in the capital of the United States. I explained that I was a U.S. capitalist doing this voluntarily. One guy asked what I did before sinking to this miserable station in life, and I told him, "I was once your Senator—you don't recognize me?" He laughed and handed me ten bucks for my re-election.

Street life in the winter of 1998–1999 took so much effort that I forgot OC and the oasis of Sarah. Survival tested everyone. But some, usually the psychotics, lacked the common sense to stay indoors when they could. The shelters required us to leave during the day—and never let in animals—but for a small price a female janitor in a building on Kansas Avenue let me and Buster Keaton idle in a work room during the coldest days. I thought rationally. I was just anti-authoritarian. But in the end the crazy and the anti-authoritarian slept in the same places.

While I was negotiating life on the streets in January, Jimmy Jeff Jones was negotiating a run for President of the United States. I didn't know him yet, but Sarah definitely did. Sarah's husband Paul Rivers worked for J3's nonprofit trade association, International Nuts and Bolts, and Sarah fell under his spell. Why J3 would ever think that his trade association might springboard him into the presidency remained a mystery to me, the Republicans, and everyone else except Sarah. Only Sarah suspected the potential of the guy. But even she never appreciated how similar Republican politics was to the basketball toss.

I became involved in this con by freak accident.

Here's the truth: I stole a pricey, bright yellow bicycle from a rich Yuppie who dashed into a Starbuck's near Dupont Circle. He didn't lock his bike. Who would take his bright yellow composite roadster in a mere five minutes? Me. If Mr. Yup was stupid enough to leave it unlocked, I was smart enough to liberate it. I never felt a twinge of guilt.

For a week during a January warm snap, I became one with the bike—working out, riding from Kansas Avenue to Lafayette Park, visiting the

Virginia countryside, riding the C&O Canal trail, feeling free and happy. While spinning madly one clear, beautiful day in Rock Creek Park, I climbed a hill when suddenly, in divine retribution for the theft, one of the $350 pedals flew out from under my two gauche feet and took me down. The bike fell on me, and the stem of the pedal penetrated two inches into my leg. Although I hadn't put much stock in things I couldn't see or touch, I admitted that God had poked me in an obvious warning. I didn't want to believe in a God that caused so much misery on the streets, but I understood that the Big Guy did communicate forcefully once in a while. Maybe I couldn't see the invisible or hear the silent, but I sure as hell felt that stem.

As I lay in the street bleeding, the only spirituality going through my head—and the rest of my nervous system—was the pain in my leg and how to stop it. When I pushed off the bike, the hole reminded me of a gunshot wound one of my homeless friends took for ripping off a plainclothes cop.

Good Samaritans with cell phones stopped, and in a concerto of concern called 911. Without an address or health insurance, I knew the police would size me up and shuffle me off to the slammer for stealing the bike. It was a good bike—except for the yellow color and the defective $350 pedal—but definitely not worth a trip to jail.

Then, in another act of God, Sarah appeared! Driving her Mercedes along Rock Creek Parkway to her home in Georgetown, she saw the commotion, my face in the center of it, and stopped. She didn't say much as she wrestled with whether to take me back into her life. Nevertheless, she stepped forward. "I've seen him before," she explained to one of the joggers helping me. Oh yeah, she'd seen me all right.

Seeing *her* again set off adrenalin firecrackers. On the one hand, I was lying in the road wondering whether I would walk again—and on the other hand, I was ogling an angel. She wrapped a towel around my leg while others helped me up. I felt my toes, so I knew my leg still functioned. "Get your sorry butt in the car," she said. And I did somehow. We left before the police arrived. The neon yellow bike stayed.

Without a word, Sarah drove to her house in Georgetown—an impressive place with a lawn and landscaping—and helped me inside. No one was home when I hobbled into her kitchen, but I had entered the anteroom of Oz. Crystal of all shapes adorned the rooms. "Not that you would care, but I like the shadows and colors and forms," she explained. It reminded me of a hangover.

My wound had bled pretty heavily, but that seemed to slow down. I limped, but surprisingly I didn't hurt anymore. I worried that I still might hemorrhage all over her white kitchen, but Sarah calmed my concern: "Don't worry about the floor. Like you, it's glazed and nothing sticks to it." She ordered me to lie down—and so I became intimate with the shine on the tiles. She poked and probed and poured hydrogen peroxide into the wound.

"Who shot you?"

Shot me? True, as I just explained, the hole looked similar to a gunshot wound, but I'd been bike-pedaled, not shot. "No one shot me. The stem from the bike pedal did this."

"Sure," she responded. "A bike pedal fell off an expensive bike and punctured your leg. Where did you get the bike?"

"I stole it."

"So, a bike thief and a gunshot victim? Do you have any regard for the property of others? Are you a sociopath?"

The question made me think: I didn't feel any guilt about stealing the yellow bike. The Yuppie who owned it obviously had money and could afford to buy another one; it wasn't as if he'd saved up for years. On the other hand, I didn't have any money. Hell, I couldn't even afford an inner tube. Maybe I *was* a sociopath.

Sarah wasn't finished. "What kind of person are you?"

What kind of person was I?

"I'll tell you what kind of person you are. You're a con man. I threw you out last summer because I learned you were homeless, that you knew every jail from DC to OC, that you cheated people on the boardwalk and in the arcades. You lied about everything, including the jewelry I bought from you. You didn't even make it."

"I made the jewelry you bought. I didn't make the matching navel and nose ring set, but I did make your jewelry."

"I don't trust you." She remained mute for a minute. "I'm going to clean this ugly wound and then dump you at a hospital. You need antibiotics and the bullet removed. Until you learn to work honestly and cooperate with authority, you're doomed. So I want nothing to do with you."

Finally I protested. "But I missed you every day. Sarah—you were the only good thing in my life."

This must have penetrated her thinking ever so slightly because she became silent again. "You use cheap words—just what I'd expect from a con man. What do you know of goodness?" She stared at me now. "You're dirty. You're just a different person. You're a crazy homeless person."

She continued to gape but finally said, "Before I haul you to the hospital, go take a shower and get cleaned up. I'll show you."

I limped through Oz—careful not to bleed on anything—taking note of the kaleidoscopic colors, the shadowy patterns, the pictures on the walls, the awards she'd earned. Sarah was clearly a hotshot Republican, close to Reagan and Bush, Sr., and the GOP leadership in Congress.

"You really *are* a politico," I said.

"You didn't believe me? Your blood is red—*I* bleed Republican."

"You're for the rich?"

"I'm for the country."

"Which country?" I asked. "The lily-white one that lives here in Georgetown or the one on the streets?"

"You're here, aren't you?"

"Not for long, apparently."

"If you worked and showed some discipline, you could live like this, too."

"Did you work to get this, or did you marry someone with money?"

I'd hit a nerve, and Sarah blanched. "Look, Jason Smith—a/k/a Smitty, homeless person, thief, sociopath—everyone has a chance to do well in America. You don't try. You think freedom is chaos."

"And you think freedom means conforming to those who think like you."

"We choose communities," she argued. "I'm not a conformist. We have a community of interests."

"So do the homeless. Who are more free?"

"Maybe the homeless, but 'free to starve,' as Lenin said." Sarah surprised me with her reference to Lenin. "Listen to me, Smitty, you're not stupid; you might have a chance before you destroy your remaining brain cells. If I found you a real job, would you take it? Would you behave, go to work on time, do what your boss told you without a fight? Can you be honest enough not to steal money or bikes or jewelry or anything?"

I compressed my leg as a diversion. Was Sarah offering a real chance to get off the streets?

"What sort of job?"

"What difference does it make? Anything is better than what you do." She stalled—then realized her mistake. "OK, come on, let's go to the hospital now. You're not worth the effort."

And then I realized my mistake. "Wait," I said. "OK, I'll think about it."

"Don't think long—I don't know if I can find you a job anyway. Who would take you? You're not exactly qualified for brain surgery." Suddenly the slightest grin came to Sarah's mouth.

"Why are you smiling?" I asked.

"Because I thought of something for an unqualified amoral sociopath."

"Such as?"

"Politics."

"I don't know anything about politics. What would I do in politics?"

"I don't know. Maybe run for office." She stared at the shadows and colors from the crystal. "No, that's too much to expect—although you're probably overqualified for Congress." She lowered her head in contemplation. "OK, you'll *help* a candidate run for office. Everyone needs staff in an election, especially staff that doesn't ask for a big salary. And I know a candidate—he's *perfect!*"

"Perfect for what?"

"Perfect for you. Perfect in general."

And so, Sarah Rivers gave birth to my connection with J3.

IV

We didn't go to the hospital. Sarah at last accepted that no one had taken a pot-shot at me. She made me swallow antibiotics. I soaked in the shower, shaved, and she cut my hair while I sat nearly naked in her bathroom. Cleaned up beyond self-recognition, she drove me to Wal-Mart to buy political clothes in the big and tall section.

The police never arrested me for bike theft.

As always, Sarah was good to her word. When Paul came home from work, I greeted him with a new haircut, a bandage beneath my Wal-Mart duds, and a big smile on my face. "Hey, Paul, I just flew in. How are things?"

Paul scowled. "Who the hell are you?"

Sarah introduced me as Jason Smith from Indiana. Paul fortunately failed to connect the thousand points of light, and Sarah ignored our sexual history in Ocean City or the bike theft or the pedal accident or anything the least bit squirrelly about my background. I'd never traveled farther west than West Virginia in my whole life. In no time Paul asked about the museums and golf courses in Bloomington, but Sarah cut him short by announcing that she'd hired me as a new staff member for J3's presidential campaign.

Paul showed no more than a passing interest, but he raised an eyebrow when Sarah informed him I would stay until I found my own place. Nevertheless, Paul had more important things on his mind than my temporary residence, including how to stop the Chinese from stealing the intellectual property of Nuts and Bolts.

My new wardrobe felt good; clothes really do make the man. Stuff an unchosen into a tuxedo, and he becomes Frank Sinatra. Strip Frank Sinatra, and no one hears him wail. Wal-Mart didn't give me all the marks of a middle-class life—such as a car and driver's license, health insurance, a mortgage, tele-vision, a computer, and a wife, kids, and dog. (Where was Buster Keaton?) But

I now had a warm place to sleep and a good feeling that Sarah would make positive things happen.

Despite my lack of conscience, I pondered its meaning, which, I had read, forced people to live for more than the moment. I realized that, like the tin man or the scarecrow, I might get a missing trait—in my case a superego—if I helped Sarah follow the GOP brick road. I wanted to help her anyway because, first, she was a meal ticket worth preserving. Second, she had a screwy, but intriguing Republican view of the world. Third, I physically towered over her, so I could protect her while she protected me. And, finally, I liked her.

While my underdeveloped conscience chirped like a newborn chickadee, Sarah and I glossed over our previous sexual behavior. However, we soon slithered back into the OC routine. It began one morning when she purred, "Wake up, Mr. Sociopath, we have things to do, people to see, places to go—and you have to reinvent yourself." She brought me orange juice spiked with vodka. When she handed me the glass she whispered in my ear, "I want to see your big nasty…wound."

When I pulled back the covers to show her, her head passed dangerously close to my Wal-Mart boxer shorts. They couldn't hide my excitement, but she remained calm and was slower to react than I was. She touched the area around the wound and stroked my leg. At this point, even a blind woman would have seen my excitement. She caressed my leg until she arrived at my fully extended and excited linear indicator gear—that is, my *feeling*. She just kept on massaging until my *feeling* was feeling pretty damn good.

We tangoed then and there—and later and there—and over and over here and there. I couldn't get enough of her. Her nipples pointed wildly when I looked at her or touched her. When they launched into a gyrating frenzy—even under her clothes—I knew she wanted me immediately. We had sex in cars—sometimes not hers—in the fitting rooms of department stores, in the bathrooms of restaurants, even in elevators riding up and down office buildings. I grew afraid that someone would catch us on a video and call the police, and I would tango in the hoosegow.

Despite—or maybe because of—the fun of returning every day to the sensual Sarah, I still hadn't met J3. But I was becoming curious. Sarah always described him as "perfect"—an adjective that began to grate on me. What was a perfect person, anyway? Someone who never made mistakes? Someone who achieved everything? Hell, I was perfect, too—a perfect street person. Well, maybe not *perfect*, but pretty damn close.

Perfect really didn't exist—not on K Street or Kansas Avenue. *Perfect* lay in the eye of the beholder, which meant everyone was perfect in the right light. In other words, if a guy fell in love with some gonad-tickling honey, she became beautiful, intelligent, creative, and nice. But if the guy lost that loving *feeling*, she developed scales, bad breath, and a bitchy attitude.

The homeless understood perfection because they recognized imperfection. On one cold Sunday morning before Sarah yanked me off Rock Creek Parkway, Leroy, Carlos, and I ducked into a Baptist church on Kansas Avenue to warm up and feast on free cookies. The congregation gave us cool stares, but we were too frozen to care. Even icy gawks seemed warmer than the weather. The minister didn't skip a beat in preaching the Christian view of perfection. "Perfection," he bellowed, "belongs only to Jesus Christ our Lord. No one is as perfect as Jesus Christ. No one!" The minister paused to let his words sink in—and the congregation waited for the punch line. He then noticed Leroy, Carlos and me and glowered. "Can these three down-and-out visitors to our service think of someone more perfect than Jesus Christ? Come on, I dare one of you to name someone more perfect than Jesus Christ!"

Leroy must have felt the Lord's presence because he raised his hand. The minister looked astonished but pleased to have lured Leroy into his trap. "Go ahead, stand up," he shouted. "Tell these humble folks who *you* believe is more perfect than Jesus Christ, our Savior." Leroy stood up—but a momentary shyness kept him quiet. "Go ahead," the minister repeated. "Tell us who's more perfect than Jesus Christ."

"My ex-wife's new husband."

The congregation broke up and Leroy sat down. "You're a funny guy," I told Leroy.

"But I'm serious, man."

So there was perfection in the church—and on the streets. Churchgoers, street people, and everyone else saw their own form of perfection. For example, I couldn't live with Sarah and Paul as a "homeless person"; my imperfect status demeaned them. But when Sarah called me a "political consultant" from Indiana, I lived perfectly well with them, said and did the same stupid things as any street person, and still counted on their respect. Anyone could become perfect by projecting the right illusion. In fact, it was easier to alter the reality of a million people than the behavior of a single person. This is why JC used parables so effectively to get his points across; he transported believers from one reality to another.

J3 used illusion on a smaller scale—to snooker the people he knew. He possessed the Wizard's touch but, sorry to say, projected a boring image to those who didn't already think the same way. If he'd ventured into the 'hood in his khakis and polo shirt, the homeless would have chewed him up the way Buster Keaton gnawed on Santa Claus. And J3 would have chafed against a bizarre street culture—the inefficiency, confusion and foolishness—because the law of the jungle promoted the survival of the fittest and no more.

All of this thinking convinced me that I might make a good political hack after all. If I could get to J3, I could explain the importance of big illusions to make him appear perfect to a big country that wanted big viewpoints. It was simple if I could just get started.

Sarah arranged a meeting with J3. As I mentioned earlier, J3 was the president of International Nuts and Bolts, not exactly a stepping stone to high political office. Like every mother's son, J3 coveted the office of the President of the United States, and after six years of Bill Clinton, even Buster Keaton would have been better. George W. Bush, the reformed alcoholic son of George H. W. Bush, decided he was better—and he sure as hell didn't want J3 to siphon off any votes.

J3 had a number of things going for him that Bush, Jr., didn't. First, J3 had a leadership flair that needed no platform as a congressman, senator, governor, general, war hero or university president. If you put him in a room of rich smart people, they always walked out ready to drop fat checks, muttering, "That Jimmy Jeff Jones sure knows how to bullshit!"

Second, J3 had plenty of back-up money if no one did drop the checks—as much as the other candidates. J3 had traded shrewdly in steel and hard metals and had made millions. And he invested other people's money that he could skim in a pinch. He did all this privately and quietly. International Nuts and Bolts, a certified Section 501 charitable foundation augmenting its benevolent purposes, fronted J3's political activity—sort of like that giveaway oil foundation that funded the Kennedys. Nuts and Bolts allowed J3 to contribute his taxable income to a charity—his own—and keep it at the same time. Nuts and Bolts covered everything for J3, and J3 never had to pay any more taxes than I did, which was none.

Third, J3 always looked up without stepping on his dick. He mamboed through minefields—sometimes wearing coke-bottle glasses—but he never triggered an explosion. J3 had an unnatural knack for appearing nerdless and urbane. He said the right stuff, stood in the right position, smiled on cue, wore the right clothes. He sized up the rules and illusions of any situation better than those who invented them. He was, in a sense, the most completely adaptable human on the planet.

I put on the new suit Sarah bought me to meet J3, and we tramped down to his office on K Street. On the way we passed Tuna Fish, Big Tits, Skinny, and Little Tom. I hollered hello, and they ribbed me. "Hey, Smitty, who covered that ugly body in blue plastic? Christo?"

J3's private corner office was rich, regal, and respectable. He'd organized his office with awards, pictures of his wife and important people, books on politics and art and sports, you name it. J3 greeted Sarah with a kiss and shook my hand. He was shorter than me, passably southern, good looking for an Anglophile, slightly graying and athletic. He spoke with a firm voice. He'd dressed in dark slacks, a blue shirt and red tie and wore immaculately shined loafers. As we sat down, I caught a picture of him speeding on a yellow bike next to a familiar figure.

"Is that Lance Armstrong?" I asked.

J3 smiled. "That's when I flew to Lyon and rode a portion of the Tour de France with him."

"Could you keep up?"

"For a while. My bike was an epoxy composite I designed and built myself. A great bike—fast and flexible."

"Do you still ride it?"

"No. It was the damnedest thing. I was out riding a month ago and stopped at a Starbucks for no more than five minutes. In that time some homeless guy stole it. I called the police and they promised to look out for it—how many homeless people ride a twenty thousand dollar, bright yellow epoxy composite bike? Anyway, the police recovered it lying in Rock Creek Park. Someone called 911 and reported an accident, but when the police arrived the thief took off."

"Any damage to the bike?"

"Apparently the pedal fell off somewhere along the way. I was happy to have the bike back—but now I'll probably give it away—I can't ride it any longer. I wonder who took it."

Sarah smiled. "Some crazed sociopath."

J3 sat back in his chair. "I guess we'll never know. I hope the poor bastard enjoyed the ride for those few weeks."

"I'm sure he did," I said.

Sarah did most of the talking in our meeting, describing me first as the mastermind of Dan Quayle's ascent, then as Dr. Jason Smith, a PhD from Indiana University, and then just as Smitty. She extolled my ability to market, shape ideas, raise money, delegate, work with people, blah, blah, blah. While Sarah expressed her passion for the campaign, J3 discussed for nearly an hour his chances, his monetary commitments, strategies, and field organization. J3 feared Bush's dynastic name, his good record as governor of Texas, his support from right wing Republicans and religious nuts. Bush easily could take the nomination.

Sarah suggested that J3 consider a deal with Bush: if Bush agreed to endorse him now, J3 might name him vice president. J3 liked the idea but thought Bush would see no benefit in it. "He thinks he's destined to become president. He'd probably offer me the same deal—but only if I do well."

Sarah got pretty worked up with J3. She made her points ardently, and her face grew flush. I kept looking at her breasts to detect what was really going on—and then her nipples pointed wildly. I didn't know whether J3 or the natural exhilaration in plotting to take over the United States caused this, but she definitely became aroused. And this stirred my *feeling*.

I finally interrupted—not because I had something to say but because speaking took my mind off of Sarah's rotating nipples. "Excuse me, Mr. Jones, but why not splinter the party before the primaries? If Bush and the Evangelicals want the far right, why not claim the center and the left? You could paint Bush as extreme and show yourself as reasonable. Then maybe you could intensify voter turnout. If you pull in the lower incomes to vote in the Republican primaries, and push the moderates to turn out in abnormally high numbers, you might take the nomination. Most people are afraid of the extremes."

Sarah jumped in with support. "We could attract the Democrats by telling them that Gore already has the nomination—so why waste their vote? Come over and help J3 isolate the crazies. I can see the ads: 'Join the Republican Reform. Vote J3.'"

J3 didn't say anything. I couldn't tell whether I'd jumped into Indiana cowshit, and dragged Sarah in too, or whether I'd really come up with something. In any case, Sarah asked J3 if she and I could step outside for a minute to discuss strategy. J3 sent us to a small conference room, and Sarah locked the door. "I don't want anyone overhearing us." I feared I was nuttin' but mutton because she looked angry and determined—and I'd never seen that combination on her before.

What she did was grab my new tie and throw me on the floor for the quickest tango I'd ever experienced. We did it all in less than three minutes, and I didn't even wrinkle my Wal-Mart suit. "Look," she said when she regained normal facial color, "shut up in there. You and I will talk strategy later. Right now, I just want him to hire us."

When we returned to J3's office, Sarah praised me as someone who not only thought "out of the box, but someone who doesn't even know where the box is"—exactly the person J3 needed. J3 agreed and declared that I made a lot of sense, but he wondered whether I was ready for the work a campaign would require. Sarah assured him I was ready. "Jason will do things you can't even imagine."

J3 engaged Sarah as his primary political consultant, campaign manager, and fund raiser, and he hired me as his staff liaison. He limited her budget to contributions but agreed to toss in a few million to begin. My pay would start at $50,000 a year, plus bonuses—which wasn't bad for a homeless person who had stolen a bike from the next President of the United States.

V

Once she established me as a political consultant, Sarah drove me to Arlington to lease a two-bedroom apartment that earned instant appreciation—not in money, but as proof I was no longer homeless. It meant a new life and a safe haven. I had a lock on the door, a bed, sofa, refrigerator, microwave and stove, television and toilet—and a woman to visit me. What else did I need?

Sarah imposed a work schedule that I kept religiously. I woke up every day at 6:30 AM, took the Metro to the new offices of the "Jones for President Campaign" on M Street, and by 8:30 sat at my fifth-floor desk overlooking a glass gallery jampacked with waterfalls and flowers. I drank Starbuck's coffee like everyone else and then dialed for dollars. At 3 PM I emailed Sarah my results, met with senior staff (or J3) and polished reports until 6 PM. Sarah occupied the largest office on the floor—with a wet bar, stereo, and a couch—but she soon spent most of her time traveling. When in town she came to my office at the end of the day and drove me to my apartment—where we fooled around until she dragged herself home to Paul.

Everyone associated with the campaign adopted patterns, including J3. He arrived at work at 10 AM, met with supporters throughout the day, held staff meetings at 4 PM, and disappeared at 6 PM. Although I reported to Sarah, her absences gave me direct entrée to J3's routine, and through it I discovered the thunder of J3's Tourette's tantrums. My initial installment came during a staff meeting when his personal secretary failed to give him a message. His "You fucking-piece-of-shits!" blew out of his mouth so forcefully they nearly disembodied his head and rocketed it to Jupiter. Despite this annoying condition, he treated me well. He gave me personal assignments—such as discussing issues with John McCain's staff or coordinating events with Bush or calling a particular contributor. He asked for "Hoosier" political advice—so I always bullshitted him with the phrase, "In my experience in Bloomington…"

Money was master to J3: Money with a capital "M"—and he referred to our M Street offices as "Money Street." J3 spent the stuff faster than Eva Perón, wasting it buying people or sexy posters of himself without his glasses. J3 referred to the staff as the "Money Street basketball team" and individuals as "dribblers." Dribbling should have been as easy as bouncing a basketball, but in our presidential campaign the baskets kept moving, and J3 kept hogging the ball.

Besides, how does an entire team ask a fat-cat Republican to subordinate his financial interests to a long-shot candidate? Do the Money Street teammates all visit his office, ricochet a basketball against his desk, and then plead in unison, "Hey, Henry, how about a hundred grand to elect Jimmy Jeff?" No. You had to work the contributor personally—gain his trust like the suckers at the OC arcades, let *him* throw a few shots, offer J3 as the stuffed animal. I began to read the history of presidential campaigns, and all of them pressed the same point: identify the candidate as a unique but quintessentially American force for satisfying a common American aspiration. In fact, make the donor believe that the candidate *is* the common American aspiration: "James Jefferson Jones, American. Cough up the cash!"

J3 wasn't any common American aspiration, even if he looked good on paper. I wouldn't have compared him to George H. W. Bush, who had a nearly perfect résumé, although George, Sr., turned out to be a weak president: he refused to finish off Saddam Hussein, and he gyrated like one of those bouncing heads I stuck in the back window of my stolen Honda Civic. I might have compared J3 more appropriately to Bill Clinton; both were Rhodes Scholars and invoked "Jefferson" as their middle names. And Clinton effectively used his presidential powers to bop women—something J3 definitely wanted to do.

J3's résumé did contain notable entries—particularly his soldiering and socializing—but it lacked proper embellishment. As a combat officer, J3 chased Cubans out of Grenada. In fact, he liberated a beach and hundreds of half-naked women in a seaside hotel. J3's command history could become heroic if placed in the right hands—maybe not to contrast himself with Bush, Sr., or Clinton, but certainly with Bush, Jr., who got lost during his Air National Guard stint. Or with Al Gore, who pushed a pencil behind the lines in Vietnam.

As I knew J3 better, he really did reveal his latent talent for becoming as dull as a video replay of bean counting. He looked like his résumé—crisp from cover to cover, flat, and easily readable. His appeal lay between the lines, but some lines stretched unbelievably long. J3 could wax poetic about his turn-around skills at International Nuts and Bolts—but who cared? How much turn-around skill did he need for a company he himself screwed up? Nevertheless, the guy had nuts. And he had a bolt that attached to just about any woman. We in the campaign used nuts and bolts as metaphors, of course. Some descriptions were pithy: "Jimmy Jeff knows the nuts and bolts of America." "Jones is nuts about America." Others were less pithy: "Jim J. Jones knows the nuts of America." "J3 has nuts." With enough mechanical hokum, we made J3 look riveting.

Sarah was pretty wired about reinventing J3. He was no slouch or jabby-mouthed politician, so we had plenty of raw talent to work with. Sarah had a gift for seeing through hacks to reveal their motivations—and I had the natural irreverence of the unchosen to reduce them to a lump of humanity.

Sarah let me rant about ways to stage-manage J3. With her Bohemian impishness, she admired my evil genius, which in my conscienceless, narcissistic way I believed I possessed. Occasionally she laughed, but sometimes she turned on me: "What sarcastic remark will you make if *we* cross swords?" I told her that if that ever happened, I would remain silent, but always would remember her perfect body connected to my *feeling*. "Smitty," she said, "you're shallower than a mirage."

J3 didn't think I was shallow. I told him once that regardless of our economic differences, we shared the same free will and individualism. In fact, we could share our free will and individualism with wealthy Republicans to generate deep oceans of cash. American ideals—personal freedom, capitalism, *Money*—would attract greedy individualists. The practical obligations of America—national security, democracy, the budget, postal service—would tap into the altruists. In other words, *getting* appealed to individuals while *giving* appealed to collective responsibility; and we could reel in nets full of the green stuff if we could weave the two concepts into a strategy.

J3 got lost in our grandiose plans, but he assured me that "Greed isn't sin—it's business. All Americans want to be disgustingly rich. But the greatest American dream is having a big stick. Even when individuals work together, they're playing to get paid and get laid."

J3's views were impossible to comprehend and pretty much bullshit, but they reflected the American political psyche. He was like any candidate who says he's for everyone when in fact he's only for himself. Knowing that this paradox was baloney, we at the J3 campaign adopted it.

First, we tried to make sure that J3's image matched American expectations. J3 needed to act like a worker on a Japanese assembly line, attaching things with a delightful spirit but also convincing contributors that he was watching your back like Leroy and Buster Keaton when someone was kicking your ass. It all seemed so perfectly American.

Second, we prodded the staff to follow a similar approach. I, for one, always pretended to act unselfishly, even though I was one of the most self-centered and perfectly atomized persons I knew. I emulated Sarah's cultural loyalty and conformed to the Republican workaday life. I liked my job with J3. I earned a salary and gained a little status by playing the game. But in my heart I always lived in the fresh air. While I stood ready to do anything that didn't throw me in jail or kill me, I only pretended to fight for J3's higher American brand of greed, which I labeled "hungry individualism." I was a mercenary, a guest worker, a henchman, a food provider—but it was all a charade. I was just out for myself, which made me a true Republican.

One day I went to lunch with a hungry individualist that I'd bugged for money. We passed Carlos on the street, but I ignored him because the hungry poor didn't particularly endear themselves to my new class of hungry lunch-goers. Carlos watched me and, as we passed him, he muttered in his thickest, most illegal alien accent, "Hey, Señor, you have money? What can you get for me?" I turned toward his big grin as if it said, "I won't tell if you won't—but no cash, your ass." I unfolded three paltry dollars and then proclaimed, "I'll tell you what you should get. Get sober and get a job." And then I grinned back.

Carlos took the money. "Gracias, Señor Smitty, but you forget one 'get.'"

"What's that?"

"Get fucked."

The hungry Republican stepped back and gaped. "Do you know him? Why don't these people get off their lazy butts and go to work?"

"This *is* their work," I replied.

The contributor nodded. "I see your point." Back in my office he wrote out a check to J3 for $10,000. "I hope you do something with the riffraff."

J3 met non-stop with contributors in the summer of 1999. I invited several of them to Washington for a meeting with J3. One fell asleep during J3's PowerPoint presentation, wheezing in a putt-putt syncopation with the projector as J3 explained his interminably dreary policy on post-Soviet development. I didn't care if the donor slept or not—as long as he didn't snore and signed a check worth cashing.

We needed lots of rich friends, of course, to buy other friends. In the J3 campaign, it was cheaper to buy donor contacts than earn them, and we paid with cash, or better, with IOUs. Early on we purchased paper-thin loyalty, so it was easy to dump a toady when the market changed. "Sorry, Jack, I bought you; I can sell you." I discovered that Republican Americans were just like everyone else—they knew who iced their cake. If you could convince them you had money, you could convince them you'd win. And if you could convince them you'd win, they'd give you money. It was a self-fulfilling prophecy.

People contributed to politicos not because they believed in abstractions, but because they wanted a real result measured in money. Hell, the American Revolution didn't start with freedom and independence. It began with taxation without representation—money. Britain needed money to dispatch troops to protect our colonial ancestors from angry Indians cheated out of their land. Normal Americans never wanted to pay for anything, including British troops protecting stolen land. Fact: the British parliament imposed taxes on us anyway. Patrick Henry announced in the House of Burgesses that anyone that taxed us without our consent, including *our* British king, was an enemy.

OK. How to raise money from all of these potential contributors who hated to pay? Easy. Dangle a bargain in front of them: a job in the new administration, lower taxes on incomes, sales, imports, exports, gasoline, estates, and property transfers. Dole out roads and guns and planes and contracts like blankets to the homeless. Make promises guaranteed by Uncle Sam. "I, Jimmy Jeff Jones, promise to give you—in exchange for cash now—the key to the U.S. Treasury. Once I'm elected, Mr. and Ms. Donor, grab as much money as your grubby paws can hold."

To contributors who wanted to buy cheap goods or sell goods at exorbitant prices, we alternatively promised to eliminate or increase taxes on Chinese imports—but always to protect American monopolies. We predicted that the Pentagon would purchase overpriced products essential to the defense of the country. Subsidies subsidized supporters—so we encouraged contributors to bid on ambassadorships, land leases, and oil drilling licenses.

We fleshed out every donor that demanded anything. We inundated investors with promises of prosperity. The prospect of a good old-fashioned war persuaded some to part with their money. Tax relief seemed better; and computers, health care, subsidies, deregulation, power, influence, guns, cars, and trips to Disney World worked too.

As John F. Kennedy didn't say, "A hurricane swamps all boats."

VI

Sarah suggested that I organize smaller donors without J3's involvement so I could praise his perfection and eliminate his personality peculiarities (including his tangles with Tourette's). In any event, Sarah hated to waste J3's time mesmerizing minnows for a grand or two when he could filet larger fish. J3 needed someone big. Real big. But keeping J3 in the background with any donors, big or small, was like stomping on a persistent weed—especially if J3 smelled a check ready to pop. While it was true that in small meetings I could run things—which meant I also could lie without consequences—the effort didn't appeal to my grandiose sense of gamesmanship. But money is Money, and it flowed faster when J3 didn't mess up things with speeches and reality.

Still, J3 nearly always showed up to snare Money or, better yet, women for his 6 PM disappearing act. When his eyes fixed on a comely woman, they turned from greenback green to a devilish red—and the woman withered. Recognizing that, I made sure that the minute he appeared, I wrapped him in puppet strings tight enough to jerk if he moved the wrong way.

After a few months of life in the campaign office—making calls, weaseling my way past executive secretaries, pleading for money, awaiting responses, following-up, waiting again for responses—I hit the jackpot. The *big* jackpot. I manipulated my way past fifteen screeners at Pearless Computers and left a J3 voicemail on the personal line of Robby Fenster, the trillionaire founder and CEO. Fenster possessed so much mega-money he made Scrooge McDuck's vault look like a trash can. He bought half of Curacao to keep his wealth out of hands of the U.S. government. He spent more money per minute than most people earn in ten lifetimes. He bought competitors with the interest in his personal checkbook. Everyone in the universe knew him—except our receptionist who transferred his return call to me rather than J3. Fenster, known as Beelzebob, took my money pitch in stride and actually seemed interested in talking to me. He told me, in his dark, gruff voice, that he wanted to hand over a huge wad of money—maybe enough to finance J3's entire campaign. "I believe in the man," Fenster asserted. "He's unconventional and entrepreneurial. I believe he can change America."

Fenster was the big kahuna we were all searching for—and to receive a direct call from the most famous computer guy in the world was achievement enough. Mr. Bobs wanted to talk even after I thanked him for his consideration.

"By the way, my secretary liked your gimmick—telling her you were J3's doctor and that he was dying. Nice touch—we traced your telephone to the J3 campaign. Ask Jimmy to call me—tell him I've got $50 million for him, but he has to kiss my ass."

I didn't say anything, but I thought *Are you serious*? Instead, I said, "He has a busy schedule." J3 was pushing for contributions hard enough to chase potential donors anywhere in the world—including Saddam's torture chambers if necessary. J3 would hang me by my gonads if Fenster and his $50 million got away, but I had a feeling that with the sale of a few principles Beelzebob would give up more. "Can you contribute $100 million?"

"Are you fucking crazy?" Fenster asked with a grasping raspy gasp. "Do you realize how much I'm offering? What does J3 want $100 million for?"

"To win—what do you think? This campaign runs on Money—with a capital M." I paused. "What do you want in exchange?"

Fenster laughed like the devil. "Oh, so that's it? Tell Jimmy I'm an idealist. I just want to support him as the best candidate for the presidency. Tell him he doesn't have to kiss my ass after all."

An idealist? Who cared if he was—or whether I sold J3's soul to this brute? "He's going to need more than $50 million to beat Bush in the primaries and Gore in November. J3 hasn't taken the nomination yet."

"OK, fine. If Jimmy wins the nomination, I'll consider another $50 million. And don't forget to tell him I want a personal meeting to discuss his strategy, timetables, budgets, issues, and anything else you can think of. I don't want more than a few people at the meeting—do you understand? I like small meetings—where things don't get fucked up."

"Got it. Small meeting with only a few people."

"What's your name?"

"Jason Smith. I go by Smitty."

"Well, Smitty, you've got balls. Come see me after the election if you don't win. I'll make you vice president of finance. In fact, you can have my job. Then you can generate $100 million in sales for Pearless Computers in one phone call."

This phone call strapped me to my desk. I never thought I had it in me to dupe the wealthiest man in the world. I had just discovered the cure for cancer, flown to Mars, and outfoxed Satan—all tied up in one experience. And Robby Fenster impressed me the most with his offer of a real job. In fact, he offered me a career because Beelzebob never fired anyone except complete idiots. Being homeless, amoral, and a good liar apparently also qualified me well for a job with the devil.

I called Sarah out in Iowa. "Sarah," I said calmly, "guess who offered me his job?"

"Beelzebob."

"How the hell did you know?"

"It was a guess. You have the right résumé."

"OK, guess what else he offered?" I asked.

"Eternal life and money."

"A lot of it. 100 giant-sized smackers." Sarah said nothing because the news actually stunned her. "Sarah?"

"I'm thinking. Do you have any suggestions for what we do now?"

"Here's one," I said. "Let J3 know he needs to dance—because if he tangos with Robby well enough, we'll walk away with enough cash to crown him president. No more sucking up to every two-bit contributor."

"What does Fenster want for his $100 thousand?"

"That's $100 *million!*" I emphasized. "As in one with eight zeroes chasing it."

"OK, $100 *million*. What does he want for that paltry sum?"

"Are you becoming cynical, Sarah? Mr. Bobs is an idealist and just likes J3. But I'm sure he wants his investment back in some form—after all, he is Beelzebob. Everyone wants money. Or maybe he just wants to keep people from taking his money."

"Trade protection and more regulation of his competitors?"

"Sure, why not?"

"Get someone to research this, Smitty—before the meeting. Call some famous lawyers—it's worth the price."

I telephoned the slick attorneys staring at me from the back cover of the phone book: Schaklem & Smakem. "Here's the deal," I offered Herbert Schaklem, "You help us now on contingency and we'll help you when we win. You might even become Attorney General of the United States. And anyone who works on this meeting with Robby Fenster and J3 can witness it. That alone is worth the effort—it'll earn you a place in history rather than your ugly mug in the Yellow Pages." Mr. Bobs didn't want more than a few people at the meeting, but he never defined *few*. A *few* could have been a thousand people if we set up tables in RFK Stadium. "Here's the question, Herbie: What trade regulations affect Pearless Computer—and what legislation will float a Pearless freighter full of Franklins?"

Schaklem replied slowly, "How about a monopoly for Pearless?"

"Good idea." I said.

Schaklem promised to get back to me with a totally briefed position allowing Pearless to corner the global market in computers.

In the meantime, Sarah returned chipper from Iowa, and we celebrated our pact with the devil by having dinner and rolling around on my floor. After that, we began our preparations for the get-together with J3 and Fenster.

Normally clean-cut and preppy, J3 dribbled over his papers when Sarah told him about Robby. He asked for updates and personal dirt on Pearless Computers and Beelzebob—a task I reassigned to our growing staff. I thought about Fenster's business motives in offering 100 big ones—and concluded with my fifth grade education that he wanted government to protect his share of the big computer pie. Robby seemed philanthropic for your average trillionaire entrepreneur—but also out for the game.

It turned out that I was wrong. Mr. Bobs just wanted intellectual property protection for his secret new revolutionary miniature computer, cheap enough for dogs and cats and small enough to fit in a watch. It slid into a satellite dish to capture and send Internet images anywhere in the world. By attaching a video scanner and ear phones to a pair of Pearless glasses, a blind man could read and a deaf man could hear. Even more amazing, a surgeon could implant the computer inside a body to regulate heartbeat, breathing, hormones, and sex. If it all worked, quadriplegics would walk, Alzheimer's sufferers would remember, and a lot of men would dump their Viagra. Robby dubbed it the Jesus Computer, or JC. Paying $100 million to J3 to protect JC was peanuts. It was all biblical and futuristic at the same time.

Setting up a meeting between Howard Hughes and Hugh Hefner wouldn't have required more work than this summit, and Hughes kicked the bucket in '76. J3 chose the most ostentatious venue for his meeting with Mr. Bobs: the Presidential Suite of the April Showers Hotel on Connecticut Avenue. Fenster's staff tried to micromanage the event, but I stopped that by informing Robby that election law forbid outside influence. I had no idea whether this was true, but it sounded good and worked. J3's interference was nearly as bad. He wanted to decorate the meeting room with maroon bunting to emphasize the gravity of the event, and he lorded over everything from the water selection to the maintenance of the toilets.

The April Showers was a distinguished hotel that celebrated the rites of spring each April by allowing adult guests to swim nude in the hotel pool for the entire month. This had the effect of blocking rooms years ahead. We scheduled our meeting on April 2 to avoid the stigma of April Fools' Day and the start of the celebration, but we faced trouble convincing some seventy-year-old tycoon who had booked the Presidential Suite on the twentieth floor that we needed it more than he did. To solve that problem we bought him an army of prostitutes and sent him to the Vice-Presidential Suite on the floor below.

On April Fools' Day, Sarah and I led our workers in preparing for the big event. The Presidential Suite consisted of a kitchen, a dining area, two bedrooms, and a sitting room. We hauled in a truckload of food, drinks, electronic equipment, pajamas, and ten toothbrushes. The rooms dripped with good taste—modern art and artifacts—but J3 insisted that the gaudy feel of money pervade every stitch and every crack. By the time we finished tawdricizing the place, we couldn't have telegraphed our financial intentions more clearly if we'd stenciled dollar signs on the wallpaper.

After the staff finished, Sarah and the security guys swept the suite. They checked every appliance for bugs and enemy videos. They replaced the hotel phones with our own bugged replicas. Sarah double-checked the food and drinks and equipment and then left—leaving me a key and strict instructions. "It's *feng shui*," she said. "Don't touch a damn thing or I'll surgically remove your testicles with a machete. We'd both be giving up a lot."

For half an hour after Sarah left I lounged in the suite—so full of tempting food and booze—imagining the next day when J3 and Beelzebob would decide the fate of the world. The more I imagined the event, the more I realized the waste of food and drink: before my sorry eyes stood rooms stocked with enough juice for three hundred alcoholics and more chow than Robby and the entire Pearless Computer Company could devour in a week. Somehow I felt in my heart that I should call forth the resources of the rooms for the good of humanity. Why not spread the bounty to my friends on the street? Besides, it was April Fools' Day—a national holiday as far as I was concerned—and the fun was beginning downstairs in the pool.

I know, I know—I would suffer dire consequences if I screwed up the summit meeting. For starters, I would lose my balls—not to mention the $100 million. Arranging even a *small* party might forever breach the trust Sarah placed in me. And of course she would can my ass—with the result of no job, no money, and, worst of all, no sex. But right now I had power—a room key.

Still, I'd been homeless for good reason: I had poor judgment and no morals. But had I retained any loyalty to my friends? Sure. I felt for all those guys in Lafayette Park, living hand to mouth. They'd given me food when I couldn't find any. We all suffered a thousand insults every day. I needed to help them, too. *And* have a party.

I left the hotel holding the key and took a jaunty walk to the parks and to the grates. March hadn't gone out like a lamb—it was still cold. Unfamiliar faces occupied the grates, but I found Leroy bundled up on a bench in Lafayette Park. He gazed at my suit and haircut and wondered who the hell I was.

"Smitty," I said. "Your best friend."

"Smitty, Smitty—you do look a little like him. But my, how you have changed! And not for the better. You look like a subhuman in those sissified clothes. Where you been? I heard you were in jail or dead—but Carlos said he saw you with some fat-assed motherfucker. Then we heard you were working for the next President of the United States."

"I had a bike accident; Sarah found me and gave me a job with the Jimmy Jeff Jones campaign."

"Sarah? You with her again? She's got you connected with Jones?"

"With Jimmy Jeff himself."

"Good job from the looks of it. You don't look like our boy. You're in the big time now and you forget your old friends?"

I pulled out the room key and waved it in front of his face. "See this? This opens the door to the Presidential Suite in the April Showers Hotel." I switched to a fake British accent I used when cops hassled me. "Say, Leroy, would you and a few of the old chaps care for tea at the Presidential Suite? I've booked the room for tonight, and it's stocked with wonderful food and drinks. But you must to be out by midnight—no later—because tomorrow Mr. Jones and Mr. Robert Fenster also will have tea there."

"Are you a fruitcake?" Leroy checked me over once or twice. "You know I hate tea—except good sweet tea like my mama brewed before I got the sugar. Well, it would be nice to chew on good food, and drink some good bourbon and sit someplace warm and cozy. But most everyone is going to the shelter tonight because it's cold. I believe Amy and Carlos are over there." He pointed to the closest steam grate. "Maybe Amy can find some girls."

Leroy could organize others when something interested him—and this interested him. He led a parade of homeless—with their grocery carts, discarded luggage and dirty knapsacks—up 17th Street to Connecticut and over to the April Showers. The unchosen never left much behind because other unchosen stole it or the police destroyed it. Burdened like Sisyphus, they couldn't survive without basic stuff like a coat and socks. Extras like tents or a healthy stash of food—or, God help us all, money—made you a target. You didn't sleep if you feared some druggie worse off would rob you.

I met the procession outside the front door of the hotel. A dandified old man arrived at the same time for the start of the April Showers celebration in the pool, and he tried to hide his face. The doorman nevertheless recognized him and greeted him kindly: "Hello, Mr. Surlepont, nice to see you again." The doorman remembered me too and opened the door for all of us. We sauntered through the lobby with the carts and knapsacks. The staff gaped, and the snooty vegetables growing roots in massive wing chairs in the lobby plopped on the carpet in shock. But no one stopped us, maybe because we looked vaguely like others who had come to use the pool. The bizarre contrast of the poor in the midst of rich nevertheless stifled the urge to call the riffraff police. People had a right to enter the hotel. Should the staff prohibit grocery carts? Everyone had luggage with wheels. The staff did gather enough wits to send a bellman or two with us toward the elevators, but I kept reminding them that I had rented the Presidential Suite and I would meet with anyone I wanted. I also bribed each bellman with $20.

The guys—Leroy, Carlos, Pigpen, Sammy, James, Shark, and Tuna Fish, Skinny and Little Tom—marched ahead of Amy, Honey, Sugar Pie, Joanne, and Big Tits. Street names sometimes matched their attributes and sometimes didn't. Shark dominated and Tuna Fish stunk—but Shark stayed close to him. Skinny was fat as hell, but Big Tits had a set of knockers that sent you reeling if she turned too quickly. By the time the entire group reached the twentieth floor and the Presidential Suite, it seemed like the French Foreign Legion approaching the gates of Marrakesh. When I unlocked the gate to the beleaguered street soldiers, they slipped in like desert foxes and headed for the two bathrooms, the booze, and the refrigerator.

"The only rule," I announced, "is you can't eat or drink everything. I need something for tomorrow."

"Yeah, sure, Smitty," Shark replied as he began to bite into a fish sandwich.

The instant I let my friends into the Presidential Suite I knew chaos surely would follow, but I was determined to turn them into pumpkins at midnight. I hoped I could persuade the hotel to clean up the room and buy more food before tomorrow's 5 PM meeting, even if my friends devoured everything. So, what the hell, I thought, let's party!

Rules for the April Showers Hotel didn't exactly fit the unchosen—and within ten minutes the suite looked like a bivouac of deranged psychotics: bodies spread out on the couches and beds, food strewn everywhere, bottles opened, beer foaming the carpet. Someone grabbed the TV remote and flipped through channels faster than a machine gun until the video quit in a huff. Clothes flew off without shyness, and Shark or Little Tom took off on a nude elevator ride to the pool to join in the traditional April fun. Willie, Tuna Fish, Carlos, and Pigpen—and Sugar Pie and Big Tits—lined up for the showers. The men and women didn't care in the least whether they or anyone else was naked, only whether the hot water would hold out long enough for them. The men used the time in line to trash-talk—and the women complained about the lack of showers for this unusual shelter, the choice of food, too few beds, and each other. "Boy, you got an ugly body!" Honey shouted to Tuna Fish.

"Yeah, but at least I got one!" Tuna Fish shouted back.

The place collapsed into disaster—shopping carts reeking from grimy clothes and spoiled food transmitted a stench throughout the entire suite, dirt from knapsacks cascaded on the carpets, crumpled newspapers used as insulation filled the spaces not taken by a body. Pigpen, aptly named, slopped beer and vodka on the floors until the place smelled like a bar after a fight. The entire stock of alcohol disappeared before my eyes—bottles stashed in clothes, bags and carts. Food catered from the best restaurants in DC ended up in the same place, although everyone ate and ate and ate, causing instant bouts of diarrhea.

Modesty was a luxury for people that pissed and shit in the bushes. Even washing your hands became a bonus on the streets. If you could find a toilet, you'd use it, but normal toilet owners didn't want the unchosen fouling them. Normal folks feared the crime associated with the homeless and withheld acts of kindness. I knew, for example, that if I wanted money, I had to show normal folks I wasn't a threat. I shaved and combed my hair and stood in public places close to some sort of security. The view of the future remained short—a few hours, a day, maybe a week. If a predator didn't kill the homeless, AIDS or pneumonia might. The unchosen stayed alienated because of their poverty, mental illnesses, drug use, alcoholism, anti-authoritarianism or stupidity, while middle-class life required skills they couldn't master. Survival required atavism—combat, speed, stealth, deceit, theft—and retaining friendship with those who could beat you or deny you food. The rules of middle America didn't work on the street.

The April Showers wasn't supposed to be the street, but it changed quickly. On the street the homeless paired up for protection, and the strong watched over the weak in exchange for food or sex. Here in the Presidential Suite, I didn't want sex. Sarah was more than enough for me. I'd had sex with Amy before and she seemed grateful that I was sticking my neck out for her and my old friends. Despite my reluctance, she started coming on to me. "I ain't had a good white boy since you—and you know how much I like you." Amy was the prettiest of the women when she cleaned up—but she acted crazy most of the time. She may have had dementia or HIV for all I know. But when she started caressing me, my *feeling* responded, and we ended up in the bed meant for Mr. Bobs. Thank God Sarah had stocked the place with condoms.

Amy didn't finish with me, however. She hadn't had clean sex for a while, and she decided to share her affections with the guys—but I fell asleep long before she finished. When I awoke at 6 AM, I realized I would have more than a burning hell to pay for my acts of kindness—and for my undeniable fuck-up to the J3 campaign.

VII

If terrorists had bombed the suite it wouldn't have looked much different. Tables, silverware, plates, glasses, and bottles packed the floor; food lay on the carpet in a multi-layered slime. The prized bunting tacked up to make the room seem presidential—not to mention the satin and lace curtains—covered half-naked bodies piled every which way on couches, chairs, beds, and in bathtubs. Someone had puked in a small room next to the toilet, and the combined stenches of vomit, sweat, beer, an overflowing toilet, and God knows what else were just too much to bear. I had to get these guys out right away—and I had to figure a way to clean up the place.

Nobody moved when I yelled, "Get the fuck out!" Sure, I received a few unkind words, farting, and a lack of cooperation—but this fit the usual pattern of the streets. No one acknowledged my authority and I found myself shouting at the booze- and food-smeared walls. When I took account of the bodies, I realized that some had left, but others had taken their place. Then I noticed that the sleazy geezer who squeezed into the hotel with us to celebrate the rites of April lay naked on the floor with Amy. This was too much—the guy was probably a Democrat.

I pondered the dilemmas for a nanosecond—then realized that Sarah would kill me long before I resolved any of them. She planned to come over around noon, which meant I had exactly six hours to fix everything. But the day was also a workday and Sarah expected me to show up early on Money Street.

As I marched around the suite in my Wal-Mart underwear, like a miscreant general an army short of a command, I found no sign of my clothes. My suit, shoes, shirt and tie—and wallet and cell phone—had vanished. Now what? I wandered around shellshocked, then admitted that this place was so far beyond repair that I'd better retreat to another location for the meeting—*pronto*. In the small room next to the toilet—the room reeking of vomit—I stumbled on my cell phone in the hands of a comatose Pigpen. I checked the outgoing calls and discovered that Mr. Pen had spent four hours of the night chewing the fat with someone in LA. Thankfully he'd left me enough juice to call the hotel's campaign contact. Then I saw Pigpen staring at me.

"What the fuck do you want? Get out!" I ordered him. "And don't use my goddamn phone again!" Pigpen slowly crawled out, and I slammed the door.

It took forever to reach the woman I needed—Assistant Manager Miranda de Veranda—and by then the cell phone battery was nearly shot. I reintroduced myself as fast as I could in my best professional tone, and she remembered me. "We've run into a problem with the room we've booked for today," I tried to explain as the remaining electrons in my cell phone trickled into space.

"A problem?" Miranda replied sarcastically, knowing already that something more than strange had happened in the Presidential Suite.

"We need another room. A smaller one to meet privately—if you know what I mean." Silence greeted me at this point, but I continued. "I know the April Showers is discrete. Is there any way we can find another suite?"

"You already have the best suite in the hotel—with private rooms. We forced one of our best April Showers celebrants to change rooms to the Vice-Presidential Suite to accommodate you. The Presidential Suite isn't adequate after your party last night?"

"Party? It's adequate, sure. But we have sensitive people pulling into town—hell, they're all *prima donnas*. We think they'll want to 'take a break.'"

"I understand, Mr. Smith. They want personal privacy. It's spring." She sighed as if it were a staff qualification to disregard the licentious liaisons that went through the hotel every day—and especially those beginning on April Fools' Day. "OK, I'll give you the Vice-Presidential Suite, but you'll have to contact the poor rich man that booked the suite to see if he's willing to give it up."

"You want me to talk to the guy? I can't tell him to get out. What's his name?"

"Dominique-Pierre Surlepont."

"Mr. Surlepont? The old fart I saw yesterday?"

"I don't know if you saw him yesterday."

I crawled out of the bathroom and over to Amy and the geezer. Yes, it was definitely Mr. Surlepont. I tried to think of some urgent reason to justify all of this—something so totally ridiculous it might be true. "OK, I'll talk to Mr. Surlepont. I'm going to tell him President Clinton wants the room. Maybe that will help."

Miranda paused. "It *is* the White House that booked it for him. Mr. Surlepont is one of President Clinton's closest friends."

"Figures—the bastard."

"Mr. Smith!"

"Sorry. Well, can you please ask the White House to release the room so we can tie it up? It's probably all for the same purpose anyway. I'll take care of Mr. Surlepont. I know where he is."

Miranda put me on hold while she checked with the White House—and my cell phone conked out. I shook Mr. Surlepont, but his indelible smile didn't even flicker. I poked him again. Nothing. I put my ear on his chest and heard only the hum of the refrigerator. Mr. Surlepont was as dead as my phone. I reluctantly used the room phone, the J3 spy phone, to call back Miranda. I'd wanted her to think I was somewhere else—especially now that Mr. Surlepont had croaked.

"Well," I said, "I don't think Mr. Surlepont will need the room after all."

"Why's that?" Miranda asked. "Did you talk to him?"

"Not exactly. He's lying here, but he's stone cold with a big fat grin."

"I thought you were up there, Mr. Smith," she said. "I hope you know you'll have to pay for any shenanigans in the Presidential Suite.

"OK, OK," I agreed. "But first you need to haul Mr. Surlepont away. I won't be here when you come."

"Just leave the door open. By the way, the White House authorized me to release the Vice-Presidential Suite for you. You'll need a credit card."

"When will it be ready?" I asked, skipping the payment part because I still couldn't find my wallet; besides, my credit card wouldn't secure a punctured balloon. I always used Sarah's for personal stuff.

"Noon."

"The Jones campaign is very grateful."

I ransacked the entire Presidential Suite hunting for my clothes but found nothing except one sock. I finally appropriated Pigpen's pint-sized clothes and began pummeling everyone. "OK, you guys. I'm leaving. The police and an ambulance will be here in a little while to pick up Mr. Surlepont. I'll be back in two hours, and I expect you to be out!"

A few of the live bodies rolled over in response. Leroy awakened, and I tried to impress on him the importance of getting everyone out. "OK, man, I'll do it," he promised.

"I'm serious," I repeated. "My ass is on the line—we're talking about the next President of the United States. I'm bringing in Jimmy Jeff Jones—so don't fuck things up."

"Relax, Smitty, I told you I'll get everyone out."

In Pigpen's putrid clothes, I looked and smelled like a homeless person again—dirty clothes that didn't fit, hair uncombed, a day-old beard. I shot down the stairs and out the side entrance. I tried to catch a cab, but the cabbies refused to stop. They knew the unchosen when they saw one. Besides, I didn't have any money.

I walked to the Roosevelt Bridge and then hitchhiked to my apartment in Arlington—riding in the back of a pickup truck. I didn't have my keys, but I was able to break in. I charged my cell phone, took a shower, shaved, and put on clean clothes. I stuffed Pigpen's clothes in a bag and tossed them into the apartment incinerator. No one should have to wear those rags again.

With extra credentials and keys and my only remaining Wal-Mart suit, I bolted to the campaign office—long enough to pick up a payment voucher and short enough to avoid Sarah. Then I hot-footed it back to the scene of the crime: the April Showers Hotel.

When I arrived, a SWAT team with automatic rifles and a battering ram was assembling in the lobby. Evacuated guests, including Shark, Little Tom, and more than a few pool nymphs wrapped in towels from the non-stop April frolic in the pool, were streaming from the elevators and out the front door. "What the hell is going on?" I asked Miranda who stood by shaking her head.

"This is probably your doing. The homeless people that wandered in last night with you barricaded themselves in your Presidential Suite. I'm sure you don't know anything about this."

"Oh, shit," I blurted out. "Are they threatening anyone?"

"No—but when the police and rescue went up to find Mr. Surlepont, no one would let them in. They said they were homeless—they want to protest. It's lucky you reserved the Vice-Presidential Suite, Mr. Smith, because this is a serious incident. Of course, if this keeps up, nothing will happen in the entire hotel today and we'll lose a bundle of money. You, of course, will have to pay for it all—an entire day that would cost you $500,000. We've called the White House to let President Clinton know."

"I'm sure he appreciates your courtesy."

"The Secret Service is coming over. I don't know how the homeless people learned that Mr. Surlepont was so close to the president. The homeless will do anything to draw attention to themselves."

I handed Miranda the campaign voucher for the Vice-Presidential Suite. "What are you going to do?" I asked.

"We're not sure. If this incident shuts down the hotel, we've got to find places for the guests. We've tried to reach Sarah Rivers, but we can't find her. Maybe you can help."

Maybe there was a God.

"I'll take care of the homeless problem. More importantly, let's get the Vice-Presidential Suite squared away. We'll need food and drinks. Can you do that?"

"Sure—assuming you solve the homeless problem. The police won't let anyone in the Vice-Presidential Suite with the SWAT team shooting up the place. This could be embarrassing."

"Has the media showed up yet?" I asked.

"There are some on the twentieth floor. They won't leave either."

I considered calling Sarah and groveling, but then it dawned on me that I could turn this disaster around. "As long as the homeless aren't threatening anyone, let them stay," I said. "Can you send up breakfast—pancakes, eggs—over easy on the eggs?"

Miranda stared at me. "Are you crazy? Who will pay for all of this?"

"You have a voucher. Put it all on there."

Miranda gazed as if I had a trick up my sleeve—which I did. "All right. But you'd better talk to the police."

The commander of the SWAT team sent me up to the suite with an escort. When I arrived, reporters, cameramen, and the police stared at the door as if King Tut were about to fly out of his tomb. I identified myself to the police negotiator as a J3 advance man.

The negotiator sized me up. "All right—you look like you have street sense. Here's the story: They've barricaded themselves in there. There's one dead—a British hostage named Sir Lapawn. Sir Donald Lapawn. They won't come out until they talk with J. J. Jones. I don't recommend Jones communicating with them, but you can decide."

"How are you talking with them now?"

"Through the door. There's no working phone—they said someone put bugs in the phones. They've wrecked the place. I'd like to know how they found out that Jones was going to use this room."

"Maybe they have a spy."

The negotiator thought I was an idiot. "A spy for the homeless?"

"Well, anyway," I said, "I need to call people more senior than me."

I finally found Sarah and told her exactly what the police negotiator told me: that a group of homeless somehow had learned that J3 was meeting today in the Presidential Suite, that they had taken a hostage and were protesting for better treatment—and they wanted to meet J3. "Also, they've trashed the room."

"How could they do this?" she asked. "We have $100 million riding on this meeting. Were you behind this is some way?"

"Of course not," I lied. "Why would I sabotage something as important as this? I was the one who got Robby to commit his money."

"J3 can't go up there today," she stated flatly. "And Fenster will explode if the media learns about this meeting."

"I've solved the problem," I explained. "The April Showers has a Vice-Presidential Suite. I've booked the room—Mr. Bobs won't know the difference—I never told his office which room we'd use. It's still the April Showers, and we can still make it by five."

"Maybe," she finally said. "Can you get rid of your homeless friends before then?"

"Are you suggesting that I did this?"

"No, I'm suggesting that you may want to figure out some way of putting an end to this little problem without a gunfight at the OK Corral."

To make a long story short, Sarah called J3 and reluctantly advised meeting with the homeless to resolve the crisis. I launched the first spin on the event by advising the gathering press that J3's concerns for the poor made him the logical candidate to negotiate. When J3 arrived with his security detail and a police escort—and a tower of pancakes, eggs, orange juice, coffee, and muffins for the reporters and cameramen, Secret Service, police and the barricaded homeless—everyone treated him as if he already had won the presidency.

With the cameras rolling, J3 knocked on the door and Leroy answered. Leroy winked at me—and then J3 and two bodyguards entered with the food. By cell phone, J3 straightened out the Surlepont misunderstanding, testifying that Mr. Surlepont had earned his smile the old fashioned way. J3 secured an assurance that the police would transport the unchosen to a shelter without any arrests. J3 promised to send the shelter food, blankets, clothes, knapsacks and lots of money. At high noon, J3 walked out of the suite with the culprits in tow. Pigpen emerged first, wearing Mr. Surlepont's pants and jacket. As Leroy passed outside the doorway, he said, "Hello, Mr. Smith, it's nice to see you again." Amy seemed self-conscious by the results of her send-off of Mr. Surlepont—but smiled nevertheless. Carlos gloated and said, "*Sí*, Smitty, some Republicans have *cajones*."

When the police retrieved Mr. Surlepont's shit-eating-grin body and combed through the mess the homeless left, they found the remains of my wallet. "How did this get in here?" one of the cops asked me.

"I probably dropped it yesterday when we were preparing the room for the big meeting today. Sometimes when I take a dump it falls out of my pocket." That comment ended any further inquiry.

"Well, I'm sure one of those guys is using your credit cards."

I'm sure he was right—but it actually was Sarah's credit card. Sarah stopped the account but not before Carlos Rodriguez dropped a couple thousand dollars on a naked swim in the hotel and meals for some of his new bathing friends.

The reporters interviewed J3 and the homeless as they dispersed. They told the same story: The homeless condition embarrassed Washington and the nation. J3 had become their hero as the first presidential candidate ever to express concern about this gaping hole in the American safety net. Leroy told the press that President Clinton had refused to talk to them. He considered Jones the best conservative since Ronald Reagan. "We want R2 back."

"He can't run again," one of the reporters told him.

"Says who?"

"Says the Constitution of the United States. You only get two terms."

"Fuck the Constitution. What has it done for the homeless?"

With the possible exception of the demise of Mr. Surlepont, the publicity was incredibly positive—and the campaign couldn't have paid for the press even if Beelzebob had coughed up his $50 million. J3 was perfect.

With that crisis nearly over, Sarah and I turned our attention to Mr. Bobs and the on-again meeting.

VIII

In something like a full court press with thirty dribblers, we raced to put the Vice-Presidential Suite together in time for the meeting between J3 and Fenster. Although Sarah and I stumbled over the joint staff from the April Showers and the J3 campaign, we managed to complete everything. Sarah and I returned to Money Street for a short nap.

Shortly before the 5 PM meeting, as we all walked to the hotel, Sarah and I briefed J3 about Mr. Bobs. With the national and local media blaring news about the homeless standoff and J3's personal courage, fans on the streets waved and shook his hands. Even the unchosen applauded.

"Don't sell your soul!" Sarah instructed him. "But be humble." We all knew that J3 needed Beelzebob's $50 million to charge through the primary process and the remaining $50 million to dominate the election.

Herb Schaklem had sent me an analysis of the trade laws. We'd pretty much convinced ourselves that Mr. Bobs wanted tariffs to thwart Pearless competitors. Schaklem & Smakem gave us a money-back guarantee in writing that their trade legislation could shut out foreigners from the U.S. markets forever. J3 agreed that an old-fashioned monopoly had merit. Why not squeeze consumers for the benefit of Beelzebob, especially if he handed over $50 million to Money Street? Maybe we should outlaw Wal-Mart and force Americans to produce their own goods. Campaign ads could promote American SUVs that didn't break down after 10,000 miles, chug 104 octane gasoline, or require maintenance costing four times the world average.

Unfortunately, J3 was on a fool's errand—because Fenster wasn't anti-foreign. J3 had never opened a can of soup, let alone a computer, so he hadn't inspected the Asian components in his own Pearless. Had he peered inside, he would have discovered that Schaklem's proposed trade laws would have banned Robby-Bobby's builders from the box. Cheap foreign labor already had decimated American manufacturing, and there wasn't much American in *any* Pearless computer left to defend. In fact, Mr. Bobs had written articles claiming that trade restrictions protected things that didn't need protection—such as efficiencies.

J3 faced another issue certain to come up in the meeting: defining his place on the political spectrum. J3 pursued moderation, but he grumbled that the GOP might boot him out of the remaining primaries because his ideology spanned too much of the center-left continuum. With the Republican Convention only months away, J3 had to define himself better, win more of the primaries, and outdistance Bush. Where did Fenster's politics fit?

We arrived half an hour ahead of time. J3 seemed upbeat. Thirty people waited in the hotel, now cleared of the unwashed except Carlos who still occupied the swimming pool and was using Sarah's credit card with abandon. Schaklem fetched five fiery-eyed attorneys ready to grovel. The hotel assigned us a platoon of waiters and bartenders to augment our own staffers and bodyguards. Just before we rode the elevator to the VP Suite, Sarah's husband showed up with their laundry. Paul and his clothes hung around as we took account of the suits.

Sarah reminded us that Beelzebob wanted a "small" meeting. I sent the ass-kissing attorneys to the Presidential Suite and the unknowns to the swimming pool and asked them all to wait for us. Paul and his laundry rode with us to the VP Suite. J3 liked the layout of the suite—drinks, food, comfortable chairs, a table, lots of help—and dropped into a soft sofa.

Fenster arrived at the hotel in a black limousine adorned with the crest of a big, red Bartlett pear, and flanked by a staff of twenty. The doormen greeted the entourage, but Beelzebob, wearing a black suit and red tie, sauntered in with only an astoundingly beautiful, tall blonde, dressed in white, by the name of Liz. With her stunning visage and Versace, Liz could have ventured into and out of Vogue. Miranda de Veranda welcomed them and escorted them to the VP Suite. Fenster seemed too young for his wealth—mid-forties, as I estimated. His hefty gut caused him to move with some effort. His dark eyes, fringed by red, tended to make plain his purpose; they honed in on you like a security camera. They sized you up in a silicon second, forwarded the results to his brain, and then reacted with a two-second blink. He reminded me of his computers.

Mr. Bobs obviously controlled people—including Liz, who dogged his every step. She was so exquisite that even Sarah looked dumpy in comparison. Liz grasped her overpowering effect on others—or at least on me—because she beamed the most mouth-watering tractor rays in my direction. I couldn't take my eyes off of her as she took a seat, but she obviously was used to stares. She soon ignored me for the VP portraits of Walter Mondale, Dan Quayle and "Cactus Jack" Garner, who described the vice presidency as "not worth a bucket of warm piss."

Without a formal introduction, Mr. Bobs called J3 *Jimmy*, skipping the necessary Jimmy *Jeff*. Using only *Jimmy* was like calling Superman *Super*, and it nearly triggered a Tourette's attack in J3. Fenster told me in his raspy laugh that I cleaned up well, leading me to believe he knew my street background. "This place is OK, I guess," he announced. "At least you made it a small meeting—only ten people instead of the police, reporters, attorneys and the homeless convention I saw on the news. I liked the way you handled the situation, *Jimmy*; but it's too bad that hostage situation tainted the Presidential Suite."

I snorted, "Mr. Surlepont wasn't a hostage—he died of natural over-exuberance."

"Too much sex, you mean," Mr. Bobs replied. "I knew the guy. I paid him over the years for his influence. He needed to keep his pants on."

J3 rolled his eyes. "Maybe there's a deeper meaning in all of this."

That comment caused Mr. Bobs to inspect the room. "Let's see—you've moved from the Presidential Suite to the *Vice*-Presidential Suite. Could that deeper meaning reflect your intentions, *Jimmy*? Are you thinking of accepting an offer to become VP?"

"Maybe *you* would think the VP slot was open," I suggested. Sarah gasped—but not Fenster or the beautiful blonde.

Mr. Bobs turned toward J3. "Are you offering me the VP position if you win?" Silence. "Well, maybe I need to give you $500 million."

Everyone laughed, but events took an unexpected turn. J3's eyes brightened as he considered that he really might reel in a sugar daddy. "We'll have to discuss it. Smitty can't offer the vice presidency."

Robby-Bobby shook his head. "But you can. You know, it's not a bad idea. What do you think, Liz?"

Liz thought for a moment, smiled, and then glanced seductively at me. "I like Mr. Smith's suggestion, Mr. Jones. I think, Robby, you would make a fine vice president in the service of a great President James Jefferson Jones."

J3 didn't react to the off-focus fawning as I expected—even when this gorgeous woman appealed to his perfect *suckerness*. More surprising, J3 kept his own eyes on Sarah. In fact, I seemed to be the only one that got that lovin' *feel-*

ing for Liz. J3 and Mr. Bobs bantered while I catatonically stared. After five minutes, the conversation halted when J3 invited everyone to feed their faces.

Sarah, Paul, and I kept out of the way; but the big bribe revived our attention. "I have a check for $50 million," Robby-Bobby announced. "I want to contribute it to the Jones campaign, but first I want to feel comfortable with your positions."

J3 tried to control his glee. "That's very gracious of you and will help the campaign. We've settled on a number of positions, but we want our major supporters—such as you—to suggest additional ideas."

"I'd hoped you would answer that way, *Jimmy*." Fenster drew out of his suit jacket ten pages of positions, along with ten pages of questions. He flipped a few folios and then croaked, "*Jimmy*, let's go for the jugular since the money comes from individual shareholders. What are you going to do for Pearless Computer?"

"What does Pearless want?"

"Just the best for the country. We need to advance the Internet, technology and free market for computers."

J3 nodded. "Everyone is for that—even Bush and Gore. Aren't you concerned with protectionism?" J3 looked for Herb Schaklem, but since I'd exiled him to the Presidential Suite his eyes settled on Paul.

Robby-Bobby laughed with a rumbling vibration. "Me? Protectionism? I'm a free trade guy—that's why I'm a Republican. I don't want anyone messing with trade or computer parts or anything else. I'm not a software weenie. I don't want to monopolize intellectual property—it's like trying to deny AIDS drugs to a dying world. We survive because we're the best, not because Uncle Sam watches our backs. We want a fair market share. That's our motto: Fair Share for Pearless."

"Aren't you afraid of jobs leaving the U.S.?" Sarah asked.

"Hell, no. Look, Americans are smarter than anyone in the world. Let the Chinese manufacture the machines. We'll design, manage, distribute, and then profit like hell from them. The Chinese reinvest the money we pay them in the U.S.—and in Vietnam and Russia and Africa. Spread the wealth. Make the world better."

This comment goosed Paul, and for the first time in two hours he put down his laundry. "Yeah, but the Chinese steal our ideas—and safeguards for intellectual property are a necessary form of trade protection. Why should the Chinese exploit our ideas for free?"

"Because—you dummy—you can't stop ideas. You can slow them down to gain a competitive advantage, but the only way you survive is by running ahead. I'm not worried about the Chinese. But I am worried about free competition. Hell, I might buy a Chinese company because it's more efficient than my own."

J3 replied, "What do you consider a fair share for Pearless?"

"Free competition—I don't want any barriers to trade—it's that simple. I intend to inundate Idaho and India and Iraq and Ingushetia in ingenuity."

"Interesting," J3 interjected. "A lot of I's. Anything else you want?"

"Since you asked, I'll tell you." Mr. Bobs paused, then looked at Liz who looked at the Wiz, who went blank. "I told Smitty I would consider another $50 million if you take the nomination. I'm prepared to do that—but you'll get the nomination only if I'm on the ticket."

"You really do want to become vice president?"

"I could become president if I wanted it. I have the money and the name. I could select my beautiful sister here as VP."

Sister? Is that what I heard? *Sister?* Now my *feeling* really was having serious containment problems.

Beelzebob and J3 challenged each other like two alpha dogs pissing on posts. Fenster described his invention of the self-adjusting memory for the computer; J3 responded with his self-adjusting bolt for the space shuttle, which not only tightened itself but loosened itself. Mr. Bobs described his first computer sale; J3 described the first woman he bagged after dropping his nuts and bolts at a trade show. Fenster bragged about his wealth; J3 sang a fight song from Oxford in Middle English.

Still, after all the silly bargaining, Beelzebob just wanted to buy the VP slot. J3 more or less wanted to sell it—but at the right price. "You're a brilliant man," J3 finally said to Robby-Bobby. "You're an entrepreneur, a risk-taker, a challenger. But this is a marriage proposal. I don't want to sleep with the devil."

Mr. Bobs seemed perplexed. "You want me to get down on my knees?"

"A little humility never hurt anyone—even someone with Beelzebob as a nickname. Smitty, turn on the music."

I laughed, but then saw that J3 was serious about the music, and I put on the Bee Gees' "Staying Alive." Mr. Bobs didn't see the humor, but Liz tapped her fingers.

"We'll be here until tomorrow morning," Robby Fenster declared. "I'd like an answer before I leave. I'm prepared to fund your entire campaign. It could amount to hundreds of millions of dollars."

"I'm listening," was all J3 said, but he looked confounded as he stared at both Sarah and me.

After saying good evening to Fenster and his sister, we in the J3 contingent took off. "We have to make a decision tonight," J3 barked in the elevator. Paul suggested that we buy more time to prepare a written document. "If Fenster agrees, we'll need his signature so we can sue him if he reneges."

J3 kicked loose his Tourette's: "Jesus Fucking Christ, Paul—if this mother-fucker reneges on the deal, do you really fucking believe we're going to fucking sue? Get a fucking grip!" J3 stared at Sarah, whose mouth dropped so fast it hit the ground floor before the elevator. Paul's eyes grew so big I could have popped them out by slapping him on the back of his head. I grinned a stupid "Man, this is amazing" grin. J3 had proved he was one of us: he wasn't perfect.

J3 grabbed a cab with his security detail and headed back to Money Street. Paul was still dragging around his laundry and decided he'd had enough. He took a taxi home. Sarah and I bought coffee and sat in the lobby of the April Showers. She, too, was confused.

"J3's under pressure," she observed. "He's usually perfectly measured."

"You think he was measured to your husband? He said 'fuck' more than we do in bed."

"He doesn't want to give Robby the vice-presidential position—he's using it to buy Bush, Jr. He thinks a Jones-Bush ticket will end any primary contest."

"His temper will tarnish his tiara," I said.

"He's already got a perfect image."

"You don't say!" I grinned at Sarah. "OK, what does the truth matter if everyone thinks he's perfect? We'll keep polishing his image and cooking up bullshit. In fact, I'll do whatever you want to make him look perfect—but he *ain't* perfect."

Sarah squeezed my leg. "That's a tall order for a tall man who can't follow short instructions and can't resist feeding the homeless."

"What are you saying?"

"I'm saying that I know you let those derelicts into the Presidential Suite. You abused my trust—I should fire you. If I can't trust you with the Presiden-tial Suite, how can I trust you with the president? Dominique-Pierre Surlepont succumbed last night, for God's sake."

"I hope I succumb like that. OK, look, I messed up. You can still trust me."

"It's in your interest to do what I tell you. Understand? Don't piss off people with power."

I smiled at her. "Would you send me back to the street if I did?"

"I'd send you to hell with Beelzebob."

"We'd be there together," I said.

"Look," she said, "just don't screw things up. And give me a kiss."

IX

Before returning to Money Street, I wandered through the hotel looking for J3 strays. I didn't find Herb Schaklem—but I found Carlos patrolling the men's locker room. "What are you still doing here?" I asked.

"Man, you should see the pussy in the pool. Take a break, Smitty, and come with me."

Sarah had warned me not fifteen minutes earlier not to mess things up, but here I was. "No, Carlos, I can't."

"Hey, it's great. You jump in and there's naked *puta* next to you—big tits and tight ass and looking pretty damn good."

"You need to leave before you get me in more trouble. All this shit today is in the newspapers—and everyone's blaming me."

"OK, but before you leave, come relax in the steam room, man. You won't regret it."

This seemed OK. No one could see much in the mist. I had little to say to Carlos when we marched in. But after a few minutes in the fog, I felt pretty good, especially when I realized that the April Showers celebrations had brought women in too. Everyone wore towels, but they covered very little—and most everyone sat naked in the steam. Without seeming too obvious, I checked out the women. My eyes fell on the hazy blonde sitting modestly on the far bench staring at nothing in particular. She had great legs, a tight stomach, beautiful breasts, and everything else a man could want. I felt life flowing to my *feeling* again, but I suppressed it by staring at my feet. She glanced at me and turned away. It was Liz. I grabbed my towel and left.

"Carlos," I explained as I dressed, "thanks for the company; but I have work to do, and you need to get the hell out of here."

When I sat down in Sarah's office at 10 PM, I learned that J3 had locked himself in his office. Maybe he was thinking—or eating a second dinner—or flossing his teeth. In any event, at 11 PM he burst into Sarah's office and announced, "Fenster is OK. I'm going to accept the entire $100 million—and make that son of a bitch my VP!"

Sarah's face twitched. "Do you really know anything about his politics?"

"No, and I don't care."

"What if you're wrong?" I asked.

"Then you'll make it right—just like you make everything else right that's wrong."

Sarah looked baffled. "You mean, 'Damn the torpedoes, full speed ahead?'"

"No, I mean *fuck* the torpedoes!" With a facial tic I'd never noticed before, J3 leaped full speed into his second Tourette's episode of the night. "I mean, goddamn it, you genius motherfuckers spin events to make me look perfect when I fuck up. Keep spinning."

I had a scary thought: what if Mr. Bobs also suffered from some disgusting condition—like picking his nose in public? What if, instead of old-fashioned Tourette's, he chewed the carpet like Hitler or the legs off Santa Claus like Buster Keaton? What if a double dose of narcissism caused both him and J3 to say something we couldn't fix?

J3 read my mind. "Robby-Bobby can't mess up things more than you did with the homeless and slaying Surlepont with sex. And look how that came out! Everyone is praising me and paying attention. I'm getting calls from international newspapers. You'll figure out something no matter what Fenster does. We need his money."

Sarah piped up. "You want us to justify his screw-ups?"

"Isn't that what you've been doing with me?"

I shrugged. That's what every damage controller did. Ninety-nine percent of all policy in the world came about because some pencil pusher had to explain a stupid action by his boss. Clinton kept stepping on his dick—but he still gave plausible explanations about how it got there. He messed up in Somalia and let the Rwandans commit genocide. Terrorists nearly destroyed the World Trade Center—and he failed to take them out in Afghanistan. His responses seemed coherent at news conferences because the media focused on his manhood instead of his mind. He was going to survive to the end of his term and then, like all historical figures, he would rewrite the record.

J3 grinned. The goofy bastard was finally having fun with the campaign. "And you, Smitty, I want you to connect with Mr. Bobs. He likes you. And so does his sister—she's a fox."

I let out the slightest smirk. Sarah kicked me under the table. "OK," I said.

I walked back to the April Showers. According to Herb Schaklem, who appeared in the lobby to yell at me at the top of his lungs, people were still cleaning up the Presidential Suite. "Where the hell have you been?" he demanded. "We waited in that pigsty for four hours and then discovered everyone had left. We never even saw Fenster. I thought you invited me to the meeting? Four hours of five attorneys' time? You know what that costs? $8,000!"

That was more than I made in the five years before I met Sarah. "The meeting took a different course. I should have sent someone up to let you know. It's my fault."

"That place is a complete mess—you'll have a lawsuit on your hands."

"You can represent us." (Later we did use Schaklem to resolve the repair of the Presidential Suite—and I sent him a fake autographed picture of J3. Meanwhile, J3 promoted Paul Rivers from corporate counsel to campaign counsel.)

I composed myself and headed to the Vice-Presidential Suite. Inside I heard the baritone rasp of Mr. Bobs, but he kept repeating the same sentence over and over again at different voice pitches. "Look, *Jimmy*, I can make you or break you. Look, *Jimmy*, I can make you or break you. Look, *Jimmy*..."

I listened for more, but the same phrase looped. I remembered my school play where I had to train an invisible dog. All I had to say was "Barkley, get down from the couch!" I practiced the line over and over with a different emphasis: "*Barkley*, get down from the couch. Barkley, get *down* from the couch!" Finally on the opening night I stood next to the couch as a mammoth "ruff, ruff, ruff" blared out of the loudspeakers. I jumped ten feet into air and shouted, "Jesus Christ! What the hell is that?"

Anyway, I finally knocked on the door and Liz answered. She wore a bathrobe. We gazed at one another for a second, sensitive to the chance meeting in the steam room. Mr. Bobs stood behind her. "Where's Jimmy?" he asked.

"He's caught up in a conference call," I lied as I walked in. "But he sent me and expresses his apologies."

"He's rejected my offer."

"Not at all. J3 needs clear agreements if he takes you on as VP."

"Such as?"

"First, he's the leader of the ticket—not you. That means our campaign sets the tone and you report to it. You're a strong man, but this is politics, not business, and he's going to be the president, not the other way around."

Robby-Bobby grew silent—no one talked to the devil this way. But he seemed to appreciate that he stood on the threshold of something big. His face lightened.

"Second, I'll be the liaison between the campaigns, which means you come to me before going to J3. Don't dump anything on him that we can handle routinely. You need to talk policy with him—not nuts and bolts."

"Very funny. You're telling me I have to report to you and not him?"

"That's right. You can try to work through J3 if you want—but he won't respond." I lied again. "Besides, he's not available most of the time—even to you. He has extracurricular activities, if you know what I mean."

"Oh, he's got girlfriends."

"He likes women."

"Who doesn't?" Fenster smirked.

"His wife. J3's following the Clinton path, but he makes Clinton look like an extra in a porn production."

"What else?"

"You'll need to cough up the $100 million sooner than later. We need money now because we have states to win—and Bush and McCain will be hard to beat."

"I want budgetary control," Fenster said. "I'm not pissing away money."

"Of course, of course," I lied for a third time. We intended to spend it whatever way we wanted. "We'll coordinate agendas and policy positions. You'll need to designate someone to meet with me if you're not available."

"You'll meet with Liz."

Liz! Bingo! I gazed directly at her—she was too much to take in with one glance—but finally, finally, she smiled back.

"We'll announce the selection in the next week or so." I said.

Mr. Bobs beamed for the first time. His wealth had finally bought him a shot at high political office. "Sorry, but we need to announce this sooner than that—I have a director's meeting tomorrow. Here's the press release."

"Kind of presumptuous, aren't you?" I said. I read it and changed a few lines. "You can't announce this until I say so. J3 needs to announce the news first. Then you can follow."

"Why wait?" Fenster asked.

"Because there has been too much news today. We're picking up good free publicity from the homeless negotiations. We want the media to see the delivery of clothes and food to the shelters. And we want to evaluate the Washington reaction to Mr. Surlepont's death. This announcement will interfere with all of that."

Fenster reluctantly agreed. "OK, it's a deal. Our attorneys will contact your attorneys to paper the pact. Thanks for your work—you have good street sense."

Liz handed me her telephone number. "You can call me when you're ready."

I was already ready.

X

Two days after J3's encounter with the unchosen and the death of Mr. Surlepont, we announced Mr. Bobs as J3's running mate. The world went wild. Even
the radical politicos hailed the gutsy selection—and with the homeless publicity it propelled J3 into orbit. Bush jawboned J3 for not following his rules;
Gore phoned Fenster to complain that J3 now had too much money and had
"foamed" the playing field. I took this to mean Beelzebob had disrupted the
plans of Bush and Gore. Individual Republicans, Democrats and Independents
plastered Money Street with, well, money.

Flush with cash and conceit, we intensified our campaigning in the major
states. Our polls showed gains everywhere. Neither J3, as the Wiz, or Mr. Bobs
excelled at stumping. But J3 faked the role to perfection. He said the right stuff,
went to the right meetings, appealed to the right people. He lacked the "fire in
the belly" of a Huey Long, but at least he confined his Tourette's.

J3 provided Sarah and me ample opportunity to mold his image into the
Perfect President. When he didn't show up at an event, we made up press
releases about his imaginary travels and the phantoms he met. No one proved
that he wasn't in Sarapopolus, Iowa, or didn't meet with Isaac Disguisik. The
lack of investigative reporting pleasantly surprised me even when I handed out
clues. Reporters lifted verbatim passages from our fake press releases—and the
few that did their homework suffered erudite name-calling (like "You dumb
shit!") by their editors for wasting time and money. The news media had so
many holes that we found whole new ways to hand out our half-truths.

In Barsick, Indiana, which didn't exist, we showed J3 addressing a stadium
of supporters borrowed from a Washington Redskins game video. J3 sermon-
ized, "As Americans we need honesty, morals, teamwork, individualism, family, love, strength, and hard work. To our friends, let us say, 'We are
friends'—and to our enemies, let us say, 'We are not friends, but we could be.'"

I distributed the bogus clip to the networks but altered my name and affiliation to Smith W. Jason of the BS Independent News and Views Network, Inc. The clip appeared on every evening news channel as evidence of J3's growing popularity and policy expertise. Not a single network verified me (although I'd had lunch with some producers) or the affiliate or even the town of Barsick.

J3's statement drew a response worthy of the press accolades of the HMS Titanic before it sunk—and caused Gore to quip that J3 intended to run on mom and apple pie. J3 responded by saying that he only intended to stand on them. The press called for more videos, forcing us to patch together new fantasy scenes. Sometimes we enlisted campaign workers to play various parts, and sometimes we stole rival footage and superimposed J3. Robby-Bobby lent us the tech section of Pearless to lie more professionally. The more dishonest we became, the more apathetic the media became. The funny thing is that not long after our footage aired, both Bush and Gore borrowed *our* scenes. It all made me wonder whether rallies ever occurred—or whether a thousand extras milled around a Hollywood lot with red, white, and blue signs that read, "Your political jingle here."

J3 voiced over a data bank with lines like, "We're all Americans" or "We want the best for our children." I collected phrases and cut and pasted them into press releases, videos, and radio announcements. Eventually, J3 balked and asked whether someone else could mouth the lines, but we couldn't locate anyone with his voice. I even searched comedy clubs for J3 impersonators. I soon realized, however, that I had to fly no farther than Mr. Bobs. Pearless Computers had developed a synthesizer that imitated specific voices right down to the tone, modulation and inflection. The device could replicate a voice in eighteen zillion dimensions: anger, happiness, fatigue, gargling, drug highs, you name it. Anyone could read words into a computer that simulated them flawlessly in another's voice.

Fenster sent techies to install the system. We reproduced J3's voice in passion and persuasion. I played around with Sarah by whispering stupid things into a microphone—and hearing the words come out in J3's voice. "Yes, honey, I love your big American breasts."

J3 wanted to do videos even less than voice spots—because he worried that too much visual information would cramp his style. His womanizing already irritated wife Linda, and J3 was afraid that the news media would catch him in the act. Although he publicly castigated Clinton for his indiscretions, J3 thought that Clinton was just too careless. Reporters wanted dirt. By detaching himself from the tabloid press, J3 assumed he could stay clean. A *New York*

Times reporter, however, sent us a tape of J3 unbuttoning the blouse of some woman in a restaurant—and we had to hire the reporter, the woman and the waitress at the restaurant to shut them all up. Fortunately, Linda didn't find out about it, but it was hard to balance privacy and publicity, especially in a presidential campaign. J3 needed a filter to stop the bad stuff without squelching the good.

Liz pushed Pearless to develop a hologram of J3. Visual reproduction required enormous technical skill, but Pearless came through with a mind-blowing holographic system using lasers and robotics and a data base of gestures any controller could draw on to direct J3. The machinery looked like a tangle of smoke, mirrors, cameras, and computers. An operator could move a model in a studio and project an entirely different image elsewhere. The system took time to perfect, but eventually we mastered J3 standing or sitting in an office environment, drinking coffee, or just relaxing. With voice and video, we conducted entirely bogus J3 press conferences.

The virtual J3 drew on his dazzling diversity. His image skied in the Alps, visited the poor in Africa, scuba dived in Australia, met with Mother Theresa (although she was already dead). Whenever we needed him for an ad, we got him. He provided perfect interviews, appeared at rallies, furnished faultless speeches. He was tireless. We conducted polls and changed his speech daily to improve his popularity.

Bush and Gore tried to do the same thing. But instead of using technology, Bush campaigned in front of scripted audiences and Gore pre-screened his supporters. Neither of them had Beelzebob to finance and develop their technology. Bush and Gore knew we were faking our campaign, but they barely muttered a murmur. Bush had to hide his own frat-boy alcoholism and his abbreviated stint as a National Guard pilot. Gore took heat for inventing the Internet. I suspected that our technical antics wouldn't generate any reaction from Bush and Gore unless we attacked them first.

A reporter named Barry Tass caught on to our scam. He planned to reveal that a J3 rally in the snow of New Hampshire also included Florida palm trees, California mudslides, and a Hawaiian hula dancer. I explained that we had filmed the rally at Disney World. I also promised Tass a job if he shut up until after the election. Tass obliged by penning a pleasant piece about J3's polished advertising productions.

Sarah delegated authority to me, and I hired assistants. Because I signed up media extortionists like Tass to keep them from spilling the beans, our staff soon resembled a lunatic ward. Because everyone wrote well—when not suffering delusional fits—we captured the half-baked imagination of the American people. We turned illusion into a full-time career. We told people what they wanted to hear.

J3 became so insulated that when he watched himself on television he wondered where he would appear next—or what he would say. Sensing his disconnected rise to power, he asked me to let him back on the campaign trail. He wanted to become a part of his own destiny. "Do you really want to get up at 4 AM to eat twelve pancakes in four different places?" I asked him. He replied that he could tolerate three pancakes with butter and strawberry syrup.

We sent him to the heartland. He performed perfectly OK, but he couldn't cover all the places we needed him. Sarah and I traveled in his stead. Sometimes the staff made up non-facts about a rally or a speech. Sometimes we even acted honestly and turned down a J3 appearance. When the staff finally overcame its vestigial guilt for lying to the public and admitted that all politics amounted to hyperbole, the campaign soared. Abraham Lincoln probably would have agreed with the truth of the Big Lie: fooling the people bred hope, albeit false hope. People want to believe in something, and once they do, no matter how silly, they refuse to let go. So we gave them J3.

Meanwhile, Mr. Bobs did his own thing while he continued to run his company. Liz called often to discuss tactics. I used every opportunity to flirt, but she avoided commitments. She promised only to support her brother's efforts. I did what any man would do under the circumstances: I used my political leverage. "Come to my place for dinner and for inside information."

"And if J3 wants our money, you'll maximize your efforts on Money Street and minimize your mendacious mind." Then she laughed.

As the Republican convention loomed, with J3 running neck and neck with Bush, Robby-Bobby and his sister emerged as more than an incidental factor. They traveled the country arguing for international trade and technology, the reduction of business barriers, and capital formation. As Fenster's popularity climbed, so did Liz's—and soon I fell head over heels for her.

XI

Liz and I worked closely. We flew together or met at campaign sites. Even close, however, Liz and I possessed a talent for remaining distant. But I liked her independence, and she liked my individualism. Once I became successful, women tried to draw me into their lives—but not Liz. Washington functioned in an idiosyncratic universe, and exploring it required cleverness and the art of escape when boundaries tightened. Still, wanting Liz and her incredible body made me feel different about her peculiar universe.

Liz was wise but largely wordless, and she offered an insight only when I pressed her like a trial lawyer. She responded to my yes and no questions with one word or a shake of her head. Our conversations seemed like a binary quiz in pantomime. On the road, I treated her like Buster Keaton, my smart, silent street dog that had disappeared. Buster Keaton let me know he wanted something by his whines, prancing, and eye contact. One time on a campaign flight, Liz's body language said, "I'm pissed!"

"Angry about the hotel?"

"No."

"About this flight?"

"Maybe."

"Long flight?"

"Maybe."

"Bad passengers?"

"Maybe."

"Someone make a pass at you?"

"Maybe."

"The pilot?"

"No."

"The guy next to you?"

"Maybe, the son of a bitch."

"OK, I won't do it again."

This code honed my interrogation skills. When I grew bored with movies or the crossword puzzle in the flight magazine, grilling Liz provided cheap entertainment. Liz's looks alone could knock the sock off of any man's *cajones*—but when she refused to play my games, she pretended to be deaf. She even used signing. It drove me berserk and aroused so much passion I wanted to fold down the seats and jump on her.

Liz didn't need to say much. Without asking, she already had everything a woman could want: a degree from Wellesley, money, beauty, a business mind, and a wicked sense of humor. She spoke a thousand words through her digital pictures of office workers doing handstands on an elevator or middle managers wearing computer monitors for hats. She emailed me photographs of J3 with his fly down while giving a speech and Mr. Bobs accidentally tripping J3. Liz shot me sleeping through the ten thousandth delivery of the same speech and my stepping on someone's toes while shaking his hands.

On a flight to Lima, Ohio, she finally cracked: "I know you lived on the streets and I know why: you're too sarcastic to live with anyone." She then asked whether I really went to Indiana University or whether I made that up like all the other nonsense.

"Sure. Why would I lie about Indiana? If I wanted to make something up, I'd tell you I went to Akron U."

"I already know you have a diploma from Harvard and that you're ashamed of your fall from grace."

Harvard? Unless I had amnesia, I never went to Harvard. I didn't even know where Harvard was—although I suspected Chicago from the way Liz raved about her home town. True, I read enough to appear erudite, and I sponged up every point of view. But only my elementary school principal ever parted company with me on good terms—and then with the faint praise of the Wizard of Oz: "I can't give you brains, but here's a diploma."

Certificates didn't impress me. Neither did the people who plastered them on their walls. I'd seen too many people live and die on the streets in the same ways. Rich or poor, little minds needed little space, and you could box them in with white picket fencing or cardboard. In the end, they let out a last gasp just like every living thing. We ran into ideologues on the campaign trail who sought immortality by trying to associate with the gods. They memorized every quip of Ronald Reagan but couldn't name the capital of France. "The smaller the box, the more confident the people inside," I observed. "They think boxes protect them from death."

"On the other hand," Liz responded, "you tear down any box, no matter how large or small—you're an iconoclast."

"I'm a boxoclast. I don't like boxes—those of the White House or the no-house."

"Even the homeless use boxes to survive."

"Their own." I told her that the unchosen weren't as crazy as she thought in choosing their boxes. My friend Leroy Stivers, for example, had fought in Vietnam and had medals—but he'd grown tired of the "yes, sir; no, sir." Some homeless just rebelled.

"Rebelled from what?" Liz asked.

"From a world that treats them like slaves. Even the wretched crave freedom—freedom from orders and bills and mindless work."

Liz sighed. "Why *don't* they take a few orders or pay a few bills like you eventually did? Pick a better box."

"Maybe they don't see any benefit in it."

"They're afraid," Liz concluded.

"They aren't afraid."

"No? Weren't you afraid on the street? Sure, you thought you found freedom in the box of chaos. But you found slavery. You weren't a boxoclast—you were an anarchist. Now you get up, fly somewhere, do advance work—and in return, you experience movement, pleasure, safety. You follow rules, whether those of the campaign or the laws of nature. Existence is a box."

"It would be better if nature wasn't so insistent."

"Then you would die. It's a balance. Ask any Buddhist. I hope all the homeless don't ignore the laws of nature. I hope they don't all have AIDS or other diseases. I hope you don't."

"Are you insane? I don't have AIDS."

"Good. I don't want a Harvard graduate with AIDS."

Want? Did Liz want me?

Soon enough I found out. Liz and I advanced an outdoor rally on a Lima, Ohio, dairy farm. Mother Nature let loose two days of cold soaking rain as we met with GOP officials in an unheated leaky barn too small for the crowds. While locals waxed in support of J3, I waned beneath a weather vane in the rain, straining to hear the stupid mutterings of every candidate from dog catcher to senator. When Jimmy Jeff and Mr. Bobs arrived in a helicopter, Liz worked the crowd in the barn while I dodged cow patties in the down-pour—and took delegate nominations for the Philadelphia convention.

I caught a serious cold. Normally, I never got sick—because weakness on the street meant death. But now that J3 gave me health insurance, I could afford to ail—and I sure as hell did in Lima. After J3 and Fenster left the rally, I felt as if Khrushchev's shoe had crawled into my head to lobby for a water-tight barn. I had an assignment in Bumfuck the next day so I couldn't fly back to Washington to recuperate. I returned to the Triple 6 Motel and went to bed. Liz had appointments in Chicago but sensed something wrong, skipped her own flight, and stayed with me. "You need help," she said. "But don't think I'll do this if you become a hypochondriac."

Our first night in the Triple 6 became a fusion of jokes, sneezing, coughing, bad television, and showers. By the sixth shower, Liz joined me, and we spent the next three days in bed—the first because of my cold, the second because we had great sex, and the third because she caught my cold. From then on, I thought of no one but her—not even Sarah. I fell hard.

This plunge into love disrupted my work when I finally came up for air, and Sarah noticed the effects. While she wasn't certain of the cause, she suspected Liz. My usual don't-give-a-damn thoughts evolved into "What would the cam-paign think if X happened—and where is Liz right now?"

XII

The Republican Convention approached. J3 and Mr. Bobs became stars in the pollsters' heaven—and it seemed, with luck, they would shine at the convention. Sarah laid out events like a TV meteorologist and called me constantly to check out her prognostications.

We were ready when the GOP gathered in Philly at the end of July 2000. We controlled delegates from California, the East Coast, and the Midwest. We earned more than a little respect from the South, but Bush maintained a better grip. John McCain sat on a long and wide fence after dropping out of the primaries. While he didn't like some of Bush's remarks, McCain refused to commit his delegates to us. He gave a useful interview, however, in which he said, "Jimmy Jeff Jones has been a perfect gentleman—even if he lacks political experience. He will make a great president. And I think Robby Fenster will revolutionize the business of government." Notice the future tense instead of the subjunctive—J3 "will make" rather than "would make" a great president?

We expected a hard fight with Bush—but a close one if we grabbed enough of McCain's delegates. Bush, however, boasted that he already had nabbed the nomination. Everyone viewed J3 as the underdog, which helped because people like an upset. In the weeks after Lima, J3 woke up and smelled scrambled eggs. He laid a firm foundation of farm and factory metaphors to further his position as a pro-agriculture, pro-business, and pro-homeless moderate. (On one sentimental journey into rhetoric, he gave a tear-jerking speech about throwing wheat, hay, and nuts and bolts across the wide Missouri.) These symbolic flourishes had the effect of forcing Bush to the far right and opening up space across the remaining political spectrum.

In our on-the-scene spin center in Philadelphia, we crafted last-minute appeals to those left of von Bismarck and south of Bismarck, North Dakota. With Republicans sympathetic to business, we pushed J3's manufacturing background: not only was he the president of Nuts and Bolts, he donated the royalties of his self-screwing bolt to a GOP-supported charity known as the Orphans High-Cap Stock Fund (that J3 appointed me to chair). Meanwhile, Beelzebob sold discounted Pearless Computers to Republican suppliers to spark support and new ideas.

One new idea from a company called Endrun Corporation suggested that J3 dump all accounting practices and taxes and turn the government into a money-making enterprise. We proposed tickets for the Space Shuttle, submarines, and cargo planes; selling diplomatic positions, immigration rights, visas, and naming rights to rooms in the White House; and investing in parkland. We promised something revolutionary: a government that didn't leach off the people.

Of course, J3 trashed most of these proposals since he didn't believe Congress was crazy enough to pass them. What if a passenger on the Space Shuttle barfed? Would we have to bring him back early?

On the convention floor, hot-air bloviaters scorched everything except the hot dogs. Lengthy speeches gave us time, however, to solicit late conversions of delegates. J3 worked the telephones and Robby-Bobby passed out JC laptops to delegates with the motto, "Keep the JC if you vote for J3!" It seemed to work. And then, an event occurred that changed everything in our favor: I busted a Bushie.

The incident wasn't much. On the streets, it wouldn't rate a police report. But when you deck a dickhead in front of nine billion TV couch potatoes, it takes on meaning. I'd been cruising the floor counting votes. McCain had just officially endorsed J3, not Bush, as did most of the moderate Republicans, and this set off a nasty reaction from the hard-righties. Bush delegates cursed McCain and J3. But McCain refused to release his delegates to us on the first vote, meaning they remained tantalizingly and temporarily untouchable. The race between J3 and Bush tightened more than anyone thought. McCain's votes became vital. If Bush didn't win on the first vote, anything could happen. Our strategy became simple and clear: get past the first vote and pound on the McCain and Bush people.

The Bushies followed their leader: Bush proclaimed that the Clinton policies had bushed him. He wanted a hard change to safer, more predictable policies. In fact, both Clinton and Bush bushed me. For twenty years, we'd put up with either Clinton or a Bush in some capacity. Still, the delegates felt nostalgic for Bush, Sr., and particularly for Reagan—and this effect was ambushing J3. A lot of delegates suspected that Bush, Jr., wasn't such an upright guy—and was maybe even a closet radical. If we outed him as the radical he was, we hoped his base would erode.

"You know that Bush wants a war in Afghanistan," I told a delegate.

"Bullshit," he said. "Bush doesn't even know where the country is."

"He wants to invade Iraq."

"Nonsense," another chimed in.

"He wants to dump our allies."

"Are you out of your mind?"

"He wants to revolutionize the UN."

"Sure."

"He wants to invest your Social Security accounts in the stock market."

"Get the hell out of here!"

"If we have a category five hurricane, he won't do anything."

"You're nuts!"

"He'll tap phones, steal your financial records, and introduce torture."

"Can I use him on my husband?"

I added that Bush was a former alcoholic, a deserter from the Texas Air National Guard, an anti-Vietnam War protester, a frat boy, car thief, an embezzler—anything I could think of to slander the guy. We did it subtly: by carrying big bright banners. The Bushies did the same thing to J3, accusing him of womanizing, lacking experience, lying about his patents, parting his hair backward. Negative campaigning took on a positive side.

Having no conscience also helped. If I had felt anything for Bush, I wouldn't have approved what I did. But Bush had become the enemy, and this was total war. Total war was a big game at the convention—like capture the flag. I didn't really hate Bush or love J3. Since J3 was paying my bills, however, he could be as flaky as old paint—but he was *my* paint. Bush had more personal appeal than J3 if you dragged him away from his idiotic ideology. In the end, Bush and J3 didn't tell too much truth to the delegates—because political truth, like other truth, rested squarely in the eye of the beholder. What you really saw was the refinement of the Wizard of Oz.

As we worked the convention delegates—clad in J3 buttons and carrying packages of propaganda—a monstrously fat Bushie yelled in my ear at the decibel level of a supersonic F-18: "Jones sucks!" I ignored everything but the echoes. I had a long fuse, but blowing up an eardrum shortened it. I tried to control myself, but the guy bushwhacked me like a dirigible on speed. He glared with a rage that set off my internal street alarms. Then the dumb son of a bitch shouted again, "I said, Jones sucks! Did you hear me, you prick?"

I smiled a millimeter shy of assault. "Did you say something?" I was proud that I hadn't shoved my clenching fist down his sewer pipe throat. I tried to move around him, which required a trip to LA.

"Aren't you Jason Smith, the J3 lackey?"

That was the first thing he said that didn't drown out "The Washington Post March" blaring from a high school band on a bridge ten feet away. Also, it was the first time anyone recognized me—so I was vaguely flattered. "Sure, I'm Jason Smith. Who are you?"

At that, the simpleton swung at me. Luckily I used my campaign materials to block the punch. As soon as I dropped my boxes, I knocked the bastard on what I think was his ass—although I was poking jello. It took awhile for him to get up—since he rolled like a beach ball—but he charged me in a tidal wave of human glob that nearly carried me into the twenty-second century. Still, I got the better of him. I smacked him a few times before security rushed in. Sarah went on the offensive by explaining that I had defended myself from an unprovoked attack by a half-crazed balloon. It turned out that television crews had picked up the bizarre fistfight and beamed it on national television. Everyone with eyes agreed I'd made a fair attempt to avoid the human tsunami.

In short order, I gave a statement to the Philadelphia police. Paul Rivers adroitly negotiated my release. In front of hundreds of cameras, the police restrained the bad-boy Bushie with three sets of cuffs. Still wearing a King Kong gut of campaign clutter, the Bushie took a trip to the Philly slammer.

As I walked back to our command center, I received a standing ovation. Signs appeared that said, "Beat Back the Bush Bullies!" Within minutes Bush and bully became synonymous. The fistfight confirmed that my antisocial instincts—honed to a fine outlawed art on the streets—worked wonders on the floor.

As the first presidential nominee vote approached, the world speculated. I suspected that a large number of delegates wanted to defect to J3. If McCain continued to demand faithfulness—keeping his delegates away from Bush as well as J3—we just might squeak through the first vote without a defeat. J3 called McCain and promised any cabinet position he wanted, but McCain said the offer wasn't necessary. McCain wanted a fair fight, and the only way to insure that was by withholding his delegates.

Liz and I responded in our control room to calls from both J3 and her brother. Sarah trekked upstairs to sit with J3 and phoned me every five minutes to check this report or that rumor. The first vote tally finished, and both J3 and Bush fell short of a majority. We had a chance now.

McCain released his delegates. In fact, many of the states released their delegates. This freed both J3 and Bush to pound on them—and within minutes the convention floor swarmed with J3 and Bush supporters. We advocated anything and everything to the free agents, but we portrayed ourselves as worthy underdogs and characterized Bush as a right-wing tyrant. Bush supporters characterized J3 as an untested elitist. The religious right, which made up a large part of Bush's forces, pushed us for commitments on anti-abortion, Christian values, and school prayer. J3 had avoided those campaign issues in order to attract moderates, but Bush jumped right in and made the commitments.

On the second vote, J3 moved ahead of Bush in both the Eastern and Western states; sporadic cheers went up when the trend became apparent. Bush held his position in both the South and the Midwest—mostly because, we thought, the media had identified J3 as a Washington insider. Sarah called and instructed me to visit the delegations of Ohio, Indiana, and Illinois, three states that knew Fenster and could sway the next vote. I grabbed Liz—but for good measure asked Sarah to send down Mr. Bobs.

Armed with celebrity smiles and a pile of promises, Liz, her brother, a squad of staffers, and I walked toward the three delegations. As we did, a mob surrounded the Fensters. Liz alone awed the crowd with her superstar aura and a red low-cut blouse and blue short skirt that screamed, "Look at my patriotic and amazing legs, bodacious breasts, and beautiful long blond hair!" But then, here was her legendary brother, Robby "Beelzebob" Fenster, the VP candidate, the richest man on earth. And here I was, too, a man who only fifteen minutes earlier had earned his fifteen minutes of fame for busting a 315-pound Bushie.

We descended on the Illinois delegation first. Because the Fensters lived in Chicago, the Illinois McCain supporters, and some of the Bush supporters, promised to defect. We then invaded Indiana and shook at least three hands of every delegate, pleading for their votes. Since I was allegedly born in Bloomington, we gained a few undecideds who knew my non-existent family. "Oh, yeah," said one woman. "I remember Maude Smith. She had a son about your age—you've turned into a fine man, Jacob. How is Maude?"

"She died a few years ago," I said.

"Too bad," the woman said. "She loved that old farm."

The Ohio delegation, including some of the folks who'd been in Lima with Liz and me, wanted to know again what J3 stood for, and I told them: "America, democracy, freedom, family, apple pie, pecan pie, cherry pie, and everything that's good and right." Robby-Bobby told them that J3's nuts and bolts held together the factories of Akron, Youngstown, and Cleveland; and he stood for business, opportunity, lower taxes, and less government. How could anyone disagree with our position? I told one delegate that Bush stood for gambling, prostitution, and drugs, but I don't think the delegate saw the humor and probably asked someone to punch me again.

Liz flirted with the most important men.

The Bushies also worked the crowds—but caused a different stir. Some delegates became incensed that Bush tried to intimidate them, and one guy shouted that violence in the quest for the presidency pissed him off enough to hit someone. In some places they even booed the Bushies. A Bush supporter defended the aggressive tactic by turning it into a positive thing: "We need strength in our military—we need to show the world we're not afraid!"

"J3 believes the same thing," I told that delegate. "He wants Bush as an ally in the fight for world peace. But what does Bush show in bully tactics with his allies?" Someone asked Bush's VP selection, Montana Senator Ron Durondon—who came to counter Mr. Bobs—whether Bush would buck up to a bully the way I did. Durondon, who looked like Mr. Clean with his bald head, smiled and said nothing.

Meanwhile, Mr. Bobs gave a press statement that urged Bush supporters to defect to carry J3 over the top on the next vote. Although the masses didn't cross over, former Chairman of the Joint Chiefs of Staff General Wammo Hart abandoned Bush when J3 promised him the job of Secretary of State. Holding himself like Ike, General Hart announced that he had reviewed J3's foreign policy and endorsed it as "sound, reasonable, and designed to bring the U.S. back into its proper position as leader of the free world."

Former Secretary of State Bunky Pucker, a squat little woman with horn-rimmed glasses, now a philosopher affectionately referred to as Ma Pucker, showed up and gave a television interview that supported J3's foreign policy. Other prominent Republicans followed swiftly—and before we knew it, it looked like J3 might win.

The next vote came, and J3 inched within five delegates. It now became apparent that J3 was going to win—and Bush cut and ran, called J3, offered to support him in exchange for an administration position for himself and Durondon. Although Bush wanted the VP slot, J3 agreed to name him Plenipotentiary Ambassador to Iran, Iraq, and North Korea. He agreed to appoint Durondon National Security Advisor and Secretary of Defense. With that, Bush freed his delegates and endorsed J3. J3 took the vote with near unanimity. The cheers in the hall drowned out any remaining mischievous thoughts I had.

Liz and I hugged and kissed when the results came in—because this meant a whole new world for us. Liz told me she loved me—and my knees went weak. No woman ever had told me she loved me.

Sarah appeared out of nowhere and pulled me into a room. "We did it, Smitty! I'm so glad that you stole J3's $20,000 bike. If you hadn't, he wouldn't have won the nomination!"

"Will he give it to me?" I asked.

"Look, Smitty, after the celebration tonight, you come to my room and I'll give you something worth far more than that $20,000 bike."

XIII

Although I truly felt something for Sarah, I'd fallen in love with Liz. After the convention victory I just wanted to wrap myself around her. It had been a long day—a long campaign—and I was tired and bruised from the Bush Bully bouncing. J3 summoned Sarah while Liz and I waited in the empty control room for the acceptance speeches. "I'm proud of you," she told me.

I began to unbutton her blouse. "Let's go to your room."

"Not yet—let's watch the speeches." She smiled seductively but pushed me away.

Beelzebob stepped up first to the podium, collected his thoughts, and recalled his successes and failures with Pearless Computers, his compulsive need to push technology to help mankind, promote the economies of the world, spread democracy, and work hard. He even inspired me—because as cynical as I was, I knew what a down-and-out guy could do if given a chance to lie and cheat legally.

Liz squeezed my hand and said, "Now listen to this next part."

"As you probably know, at Pearless Computers we have developed a revolutionary new personal computer called the JC. It's the size of a quarter and fits on your keychain: not only can you carry your own PC in your pocket, you can access it anywhere—through a cell phone, a watch, a television, or even a gas pump. Because I believe in the ideals of America so much, I will give a new JC PC to every kid in America who graduates from high school."

Beelzebob had committed himself to more than a billion retail dollars a year—an amazing amount in general, but a small dent in his wallet. What I didn't know was that the basic JC Computer, which Robby was brilliantly hustling to the world via this speech, cost him ten bucks. With, say, ten million high school graduates a year, Fenster was laying out a paltry $100 million a year. A JC Computer was cheaper than lipstick or a haircut.

The convention—filled with conservatives—sat mute trying to process Mr. Bob's eleemosynary motives. Like me, they pictured the ground-breaking JC as a clunky old computer and added up the costs. But unlike me, they imposed a moral code to analyze the JC proposal. "Son, you can't have a free JC PC until you show me you can take care of it."

"Dad," the sons would say, "it's the size of a key. I'm not going to flush it down the toilet."

OK, so Fenster tossed them a random bone they couldn't chew right away. He certainly was showing corporate responsibility, but now some wondered whether Beelzebob had become a liberal in GOP clothing. How could Pearless afford it? Wouldn't the stock drop? No doubt some in Fenster's world-wide audience appreciated the benefits a new computer might provide kids for finding jobs, keeping them off the streets, and encouraging them to go to college.

As Fenster explained more about the JC, delegates pulled out their cell phones and called their brokers, shouting audibly, "Buy Pearless!" Some bolted from their convention seats to buy on the Tokyo exchange. By the end of the speech, Mr. Bobs had increased his net worth by another $10 billion—enough to subsidize 100 years of JC PCs.

Liz cheered wildly for her brother and hugged me at least ten times. I received a call from Sarah instructing Liz and me to make our way to the stage for J3's address. As we did, cameras showed us as a couple. "Marry her!" someone shouted. We climbed the stage and stood in the back with Sarah and Paul Rivers, a glowing Mr. Bobs, General Wammo Hart, and Ron Durondon. Bush, Jr., took a seat with the Texas delegation and munched on barbequed pork. J3 took the podium to sustained cheers.

J3 had prepared detailed remarks, but he waited for the noise to die down before beginning. "Robby's a devil to follow!" This caused more cheers. "We should thank JC for the JC!" Still more cheers from the religious right.

Once he finished his introductory salutes, J3 launched into the "big tent" sermon that really said, "Hey, right wingers, moderates, and left wingers: although we all hate each other, we like Ronald Reagan. Can't we just all get along?" He actually stated it differently, but I'm sure that's what he meant.

J3 gave Bush, Jr., perfunctory and insincere praise for running a good campaign—and Bush, Jr., toasted J3 with his barbeque. J3 quickly turned toward Al Gore, the heir-apparent of Clinton.

"Let us show the nation," J3 proposed in lofty prose, "that compassion extends to all ideologies—that Republicans promote honest government, true freedom, fiscal responsibility, economic productivity, morality, and family. We welcome all Republicans and Democrats to our cause. Republicans may lead the way, but we are all one nation under God filled with good men and women, every religion, ethnic group, and economic class, immigrants and natives, north and south and east and west. We are everyone!"

The convention cheered—they would have cheered if J3 had announced an alliance with Saddam Hussein—and they learned that J3 intended to stake out the entire political spectrum. "As Aristotle advised, 'moderation in all things.' I am a moderate in the diversity that makes up our United States of America!" The TV spinmeisters instantly agreed that J3 perfectly positioned himself to poke Gore.

J3's desire to take the broad center perplexed the conservatives but didn't dampen their fervor. They became less baffled, however, when J3 stated, "Let the world know we will not tolerate terrorism. The new enemies of America and civilization are those who seek to undermine our strength rather than develop their own. We will stop terrorists by finding and eradicating them—and by reaching out to the frustrated masses that might support their twisted ideology. Let me make this clear: any terrorist that attacks an American attacks America. To those considering it, *Don't do it!* I warn you! America will respond to your malice."

The audience went silent again and collectively wondered: What terrorism? The World Trade Center crazies? What was J3 talking about? None of us knew exactly. But whatever it was, J3's remarks had a great impact.

As J3 finished, he introduced us, beginning with his wife. Linda, he announced, would make the best First Lady of the United States since Abigail Adams. Linda beamed dutifully and kissed her husband. J3 beckoned me. "Here's Jason Smith, the man who personifies the best of America by standing up to a bully—and you can see it by his shiner. This man is my hero. Not only did he pull himself up by his own bootstraps, he had the brains to guide me through the primary campaigns. Thank you, Smitty." The convention applauded respectfully.

J3 then introduced Sarah as his right-hand woman. "If it hadn't been for this wonderful lady, I wouldn't be standing here." The convention applauded again. I cheered, too, because Sarah was *my* hero. J3 saluted Liz and told the convention that he expected Liz to become the next president of Pearless Computers when Mr. Bobs became Vice President of the United States. "Liz Fenster is one of the smartest women I've ever met."

When the dust settled, Liz disappeared with her brother. After taking care of business, I made my way to the hotel with Sarah. Paul already had gone to bed—it was past 2 AM. Sarah wanted to spend the rest of the night with me, but I wanted to take a shower and head off to Liz's room. Unfortunately, I didn't know where Liz was. If I refused to sleep with Sarah, it would irritate her—and no matter how much I wanted to lounge with Liz, I didn't want to scorch Sarah.

Paul temporarily resolved the dilemma. He woke up and discovered that Sarah hadn't returned from the convention. He called my room looking for her. I told him that she had ridden with me back to the hotel in the taxi and might be celebrating in the bar with the staffers.

As the conversation with Paul ended, Liz showed up at my room, too—thankfully before either Sarah or I started dropping clothes. Sarah felt the sting and said she ought to return to her room. Liz suggested that the three of us stroll outside for breakfast, and Sarah agreed. Sarah called Paul to invite him, but he mumbled something and went back to sleep.

Liz, Sarah, and I wandered a few blocks to an all-night dive in Center City; but even with the heat, the attitudes remained frosty. Insomnolent drifters decorated the booths. We grabbed a free table and ordered coffee and pancakes, congratulated one another on the victory of J3 and Mr. Bobs, dissected the speeches, and predicted the future. Sarah seemed as distant as Liz used to be—hurt, really—despite the euphoria. Sarah sensed that Liz and I had developed a serious relationship. I felt bad because I worshiped Sarah and didn't want to hurt her. But I wondered whether Paul, back at the hotel, felt the same pain when Sarah lavished attention on me.

"Where is your room?" Sarah finally asked Liz.

"Next to Robby's. We're on the same floor." Liz also seemed uncomfortable.

Sarah groaned ever so slightly. "Well," she sighed as if the sun had finally set, "maybe it's time to turn in."

The walk back to the hotel wasn't any easier. After we split up—Sarah to mollify Paul and Liz to wait for me—I took a shower, changed clothes, and banged the button for the buggy to Liz's room. As the elevator door opened, Sarah poured out in her same clothes—meaning that she hadn't returned to her room for very long. "I just have a few minutes," she said, "Paul's snoozing—but he's a light sleeper and will look for me if we're not fast."

We returned to my room and she attacked me. Off came her clothes, off came mine, and my *feeling* definitely rose to the occasion. Sarah had a magnificent body—her breasts kept me busy for a month. I never even resisted. I'd been looking forward to Liz, but I wondered whether I had enough for two women. Sarah worked fast—and in less than twenty minutes we collapsed next to each other.

Then the phone rang. Was it Paul? Was it Liz? Sarah was swift: "Don't answer it—no matter who it is, it's not good." Sarah jumped up, dressed, and took off.

I ran into the shower again, dressed, and headed up to Liz's room. I knocked, but no one answered. I knocked again. Finally, a bathrobed Liz answered the door.

"You were supposed to be here forty-five minutes ago. I went to bed."

"Can I come in?"

"Why?"

"Why?" I repeated.

"I'll tell you why I asked why. Because if you want to sleep with me, then don't sleep with Sarah or anyone else. I'm not stupid, Smitty."

We stood in the hall exchanging data packets of sounds—idly, for a moment, and then in loud bursts. Our voices could have informed the entire world that I was having multiple relations with a married woman and the sister of the next Vice President of the United States. Anyone, including Sarah, could have popped out of a room to shut us up. "Can we talk about this inside?" I finally asked Liz.

"No, we'll talk about it here. I'm not letting you in until we settle this."

"You want an exclusive relationship?" I asked in a whisper.

"I'm not a whore!" she shouted. "I'm not some 'other girl' you can use. If you want me, I expect honesty and decency. You understand that, don't you, Mr. No-Conscience?"

"Of course," I lied.

"You're not going to sleep with other women if you sleep with me. *Comprende?*"

I had to think fast. If I wanted Liz, I had to back away from Sarah. I'd fallen in love with Liz, and I might actually marry her if I wasn't as brainless as I was guiltless. Liz had let me penetrate her hard shell, a privilege she never granted anyone. But could I forsake Sarah? I looked at Liz. She wanted me to commit myself. I had never committed myself to anything except Buster Keaton—and he took off. Even J3 never earned my complete allegiance. Maybe because I wasn't perfect enough for anyone, no one was perfect enough for me. What to do?

"Liz, can we please talk about this inside? I love you—you know that."

Liz seemed astonished. "If you love me, then promise right here and now undivided loyalty. You're a street person, but I'm giving you a chance to change your narcissistic attitude." If love had been anything else—politics, business, hustling—I would have known what to do. But this was Liz. She was different. I stared at her and she stared back. "I'm going to close the door in thirty seconds if you don't tell me right now." She was beautiful, good, virtuous—everything a man could want.

"Let me in," I stated firmly. "I love you, and you're the only woman in my life."

She opened the door, and I went in. I had done it—I made a real and honest commitment. But could I keep it? At least this was a question every human on earth faced.

XIV

Just after dawn I dragged myself back to my own room, only to have J3 greet me with a blue Tourette's phone call. "Where the mother-fucking-goddamn-piece-of-shit have you been?" he asked. "I called your [expletive deleted] room, your [expletive deleted] cell phone—even Liz's, uh, room."

"I must have slept well," I lied.

"I sure as hell hope not. Sleep is something you can't afford any longer. Get your ass up here. We're talking about the campaign."

I cleaned up, shaved, and ran as fast as I could up the stairwell to J3's suite. There I encountered a full Secret Service detail, and when I tried to enter, a large bulldog agent by the name of Deuce Brucie, attached by his ears to a hundred wires, stopped me, inspected the black eye I'd earned the night before, and demanded identification. Since I hadn't bothered with my wallet in my rush to appear, Brucie ordered me to go back and retrieve it. By the time I returned, J3 stood outside in the hallway joking with Brucie about the go-fetch-it prank. "You can let him in," J3 said. "He's my right hand's right hand—the one that popped that fat Bushie last night."

"I know—I just wanted to watch him run."

When I entered, I saw Sarah, Linda, Ron Durondon, General Hart, Ma Pucker, Mr. Bobs, a sleepy Liz, and others I didn't know, talking and munching on toast. Apparently no one except Sarah's husband had slept the night before, and as far as I knew he still was sleeping. Sarah sat on a couch looking weary and grumpy.

J3 took the floor to polite applause. "OK, we won the nomination. Now we face the real work of beating Al Gore. Gore will try to capture the middle we've staked out. We have to reclaim the right and retain the middle. That's why you're all here: to advise me and devise a pithy catchphrase that appeals to the center and the right—concern for people and security."

"Compassionate conservativism," Durondon pronounced. "It'll work."

"No," said Sarah. "That was Bush's position. No one believed Bush was compassionate."

"War and peace," Pucker joked. Pucker had written twenty books on foreign policy and had just published her latest called *Tolstoy's Redundant Tactical Trial of Totalitarian Tactics.*

"Peace and war," General Hart responded. "I've had enough of war."

J3 stopped everyone. "That's good—Peace and War. We need to think in that box."

We listened to the perfect candidate and the assorted opinions of those in the room. Terrorism burst forth as the main issue, especially radical Muslim terrorism. According to Ron Durondon, Clinton had botched pursuit of the terrorist organization responsible for the World Trade Center bombing. The Clinton folks knew the bad guys—members of a group called *al Qaeda* run by Saudi maniac Usama bin Laden—but they couldn't reach him in Afghanistan. Former Reagan CIA Director Jorge "Bull" Consep, who now ran an international security firm, briefed us on terrorism and described the radical cells operating in major cities—some waiting to hijack planes and bomb buildings.

"Why are they doing this?" I asked Consep. This was easy to ask because I'd learned world affairs at the International House of Pancakes. "What did we do to set this off?"

Pucker took the floor. "We didn't do anything, but here's my theory: We have too much money and power for their liking. Western individualism disrupts the religious culture of the Mideast. Moderate Muslims adjust, but the fundamentalists can't. Because they have no army to resist us, they use terrorist tactics."

Durondon chimed in. "Look, these people live in the fourteenth century. They're not only anti-western, anti-technology, and anti-capitalist; they believe every goddamn thing they read in the Koran. If it tells them to smite the infidels, they do it. They don't think on their own."

"Like our own religious extremists," J3 agreed. "Look at the guy who bombed the Olympic Park in Atlanta. Or look at the KKK or the neo-Nazis."

Mr. Bobs shook his head. "These crazies don't understand that technology sets you free. It makes you healthy, wealthy, and wise."

"If you can afford it," Sarah noted. "Tell people living in the dirt about the Internet or see if they care what kind of cars Americans drive."

Durondon shook his head. "Terrorists go for our soft spots—our open society, our lack of security. When was the last time someone searched you in an office building? Check out the April Showers, Smitty. You marched those bums right into the Presidential Suite. No one stopped you. And some honey-pot knocked off Dominique-Pierre Surlepont."

"He went with a big smile on his face," I asserted.

"Clinton wanted to start an investigation into that smile," Durondon chuckled.

Consep finished his presentation and then listened. J3 got to the point: "If we clamp down on terrorists, don't we give up our own freedom? If we shut down the borders and restrict movement, don't we look like a totalitarian state? How can I advocate that?"

"The problem is balance," Durondon explained. "First we get you elected—then we act. If these knucklehead terrorists want to kill themselves, that's one thing. But if they want to kill us, we have to preempt them before they try. Once we wipe them out, we can regain our freedoms."

General Hart had remained silent, but he didn't like the drift. "If we start a war—even against terrorists—there's no going back. We have to know the details of a war—the troop strength, the mission, the exit. You can't ask American soldiers to decipher the Koran in the field to nail some bastard who follows the Sharia. As Ma Pucker points out, this is all cultural. More extremists will fill any vacuum we produce by killing a few terrorists. People retain their beliefs. Unless you kill everyone, you don't change cultures."

Durondon replied, "On the contrary, General. A quick and dirty war against all the terrorists will tell them that fighting progress is futile. The faster they dump their backward ideas, the better. Look, it's inevitable that markets will open, that computers and cell phones will alter their lives. These terrorists are dinosaurs—they won't change until we reshape the Mideast."

"This sort of talk will scare the hell out of the American people," J3 said. "No one wants a big war. If we tell America that terrorism might come here, it will panic the population. Robby Fenster is right: we need technology to do the heavy lifting."

"Then we should launch a small, precise war," Pucker suggested, "and limit it to countries that harbor terrorists."

"We need to give Jimmy Jeff a solid position with Gore," Sarah stated. "Gore and Clinton have been asleep at the switch."

This debate went on for the better part of the day; but by closing time, a consensus congealed that J3 would use the issue of terrorism to show Gore's weaknesses. Once we won the election, however, we would take precise action. We all swore secrecy to our quest for world peace through limited world war.

XV

Sarah's growing irritation with me expressed itself in her impatience and criticisms of little things. Eventually I couldn't avoid the real problem: I'd committed myself to Liz. I really did love Sarah. After all, she had snatched me from the streets and turned me into a political hack as loyal and corrupt as any other. But I'd sworn to Liz that I wouldn't go back to sleeping with Sarah.

Liz fenced off emotional terrain. In the process of gaining citizenship to the territory, I confessed my relationship with Sarah. Liz had an almost voyeuristic fascination that matched some of the explicit photographs she produced one day. She asked whether Sarah liked oral sex, whether Sarah had as many orgasms as Liz. I realized that even Liz wasn't as perfect as I thought and was competing with Sarah—or was gathering a unique arsenal of intelligence. Or maybe she was kinky and I didn't know it. If I criticized Sarah for something minor, Liz overreacted: "Sarah is using you." I never figured out what I possessed that Sarah used, other than my talent for making her smile. In fact, *I* had used Sarah—for a job, security, ideas, some of the best sex I'd ever experienced.

I felt guilty for my disloyalty to Sarah, even though Sarah was married and unavailable. Sarah and I didn't break our emotional bonds easily. One evening on the road, she confronted me in my hotel room. "What is going on?" she demanded. "I've taken insane risks with you. You're not even married, but you won't sleep with me. Do you care about me?"

"Of course I care about you. But you're married, and we can't jeopardize the campaign."

"When did you start worrying about morals?"

"When I met you," I said.

"You're full of it, Smitty. You do whatever you can get away with—even with Liz. I liked you more when you didn't worry about morals."

"OK, so I push the limits."

"I don't need you to push limits. I could have picked any one of a million men if I wanted a real psychopath."

We stared at each other with that look Buster Keaton saved for dogs he didn't trust. I had to admit that Sarah had been incredibly good to me—and in payment I'd caused her pain. We were alone, and no one knew what we might do—certainly not Liz. "What do you want, Sarah?"

"I want you, you dumb son of a bitch."

"More than Paul? More than this life you lead? What do I offer you? I'm unchosen. Remember?"

"You're not unchosen now. I'm choosing you."

So much for my promise to Liz—we ended up in bed. Sarah had a way about her that my body couldn't resist. "How's your *feeling*?" she asked, knowing full well. My *feeling* had a mind of its own—especially around her. As I learned on the streets, "When one head gets soft, the other gets hard." Who needed drugs when I had Sarah?

"What about Paul?" I asked after we finished choosing one another.

"What about him?" she answered. "Our married life is horrible. He and I have different schedules. *He's* sleeping with his secretary. It's all a big Mexican hat fuck."

"Mexican hat fuck? Did you just make that up?"

Sarah laughed. "J3 invented it during one of his Tourette's rages. But I liked it."

"How would you and J3 have a conversation about fucking? Are you sleeping with him?"

"I just told you he went off on a rage."

Something was fishy. "You are sleeping with him, aren't you?"

"No longer. I slept with him when I started having trouble with Paul. Why do you think he put me on the campaign? How do you think I got you on it?"

"The Perfect President cheated with you, too?"

Sarah said nothing for a few seconds. "Do you hate me?"

"No, I don't hate you." In fact, I felt better because my guilt instantly disappeared. It made me think how similar everyone was. "On the street, Carlos and Big Tits sell their bodies for money and drugs; but they pair up for protection. The White House is just across the tracks from Lafayette Park."

"But *we* have moral values." Even Sarah laughed at her outlandish statement. This sort of morality meant living by your own rules, no matter how bizarre your game. Every two-bit dictator believed in divine law. Sarah stared at my wise-ass smirk. "You may worship Liz. But she's into Mexican hat dances, too—and not just with sex."

"No. She really is different."

"She'll dump you. So don't get too comfortable."

When we returned to Money Street, I heard the Mexican trumpets. J3, Mr. Bobs, Bush, Durondon, General Hart, and the whole political mariachi band boogied around a big power sombrero as November approached. We paid the *gaiteros* for their truth: "You can't win if you don't dance." The opposite, however, seemed more apt: "You can't dance if you don't win." Winning drove us—nothing else mattered. We hired pollsters to measure every gyration. We changed positions like Cancun day-traders punching at piñatas.

Then, in a flash of brilliance, I realized how easy it was to match the voter's view with ours. We would increase the demand for J3 ideology by limiting the sombrero supply. If we spit out bits of seductive information—facts and opinions not exactly garbage, but close—the public would clamor for more because it had no alternative. It was classic advertising! Or better, we were creating a jigsaw puzzle where only a few pieces fit. I called this "selection"—but privately I knew it was just propaganda.

Sarah and I dumped "Peace and War" in favor of "Domestic and Foreign Strength." We conveyed that internal security meant more to J3 than foreign policy. President Jones would look inward to rid the nation of rotten elements and then outside at the enemies at the gate. This policy appealed to the paranoids and reinforced our attacks on the weak anti-terrorist policies of Clinton and Gore.

The more we rearranged reality, the more we improved in the polls. J3 rose as a defense leader—and a person who reacted to foreign problems by building walls. In our piles of polls, we learned that voters valued leadership more if they felt fear. J3's numbers therefore climbed among the paranoids but fell among poor folks who preferred a war on poverty to a war on a distant evil. However, our polls showed that alienated people (like me) bitched but rarely voted. I didn't want to abandon the bitching poor—and especially the bitching voting poor—so Sarah and I pulled up Bush's rejected word "compassion" to stir the masses and used it as "Jones—Compassionate and Strong." The poll numbers reacted positively.

Eventually I realized that *words* mattered more than numbers. Words had the power to focus attention—so we hired marketing gurus to spit out spiky sayings whenever the polls flickered. While the press called these guys spin-doctors, we called them the emergency medical team—the EMT—since we couldn't wait for appointments.

I received an email accusing J3 of setting up a propaganda ministry, which was true. Like most of us with no sense of right and wrong, J3 pursued idealistic ends that justified dubious means. J3 did set moral limits, however. He didn't like personal violence or singling out ethnic groups, even though he erupted into a full-tic Tourette's tantrum at Eskimos for killing baby seals. "Those blubber-eating bastards ought to learn to eat tacos, hummus, and pasta like normal Americans." We recognized that you could push people only so far with words. If you really wanted to manipulate the electorate, you had to act. We tried to imagine some awe-inspiring event to showcase J3's leadership—a disaster that would attract the rubberneckers of the world.

XVI

God might have supplied the disaster, but I found no evidence of His intent to create more chaos in the campaign. I couldn't dispute the divine purposes trumpeted by the holy rollers for J3's emergence, but their shrill voices did get tiring. I assumed that God was on our side—but I wasn't exactly sure which side that was. God probably watched the pandemonium from some comfortable cloud; but it seemed the closer J3 got to the White House, the more our religious advisers felt He came down to earth to rule on every issue. I personally attracted a special God squad that expressed concern with my irreverence. It tried to persuade J3 to curtail my cheekiness, but Sarah replied for J3 that without God's hand I might still be wandering the streets aimlessly with Buster Keaton—if I could find him again. Somehow, Sarah wrote, God had led me to influence the world through J3. So God definitely had a sense of humor.

I bought a video of *The Wizard of Oz* to remind myself of the power of blind faith. If people thought you had power, you had it—you could do crazy things. As Dorothy discovered, illusions gave more hope than reality, which all kids in the world understood. For the campaign, casting illusions had become a major component. The EMTs generated an endless spring of fancy, all to dupe the munchkins into believing J3 would become president regardless of anything the wicked witch of the left—Al Gore—said or did.

Gore also used illusions, as we learned from Flack-Jack MacDonald, an eighteen-year-old college freshman intent on becoming the next Richard Nixon. He defected from Gore's camp with a staff manual and debate preparation books. Gore apparently had his own EMTs, although he called them the FARM—For American Reform of Mankind. We read in the manual of young MacDonald that the "Economic Intent to Extract Income Organization"—or the EIEIO—shaped Gore's FARM policy. Gore spewed an open fire hydrant of unending policy of one-for-all and all-for-one. We had religious zealots, but

Gore attracted rich do-gooders, commies, and an intergalactic welcoming committee, all wanting perfect equality. Gore went farther than Karl Marx: From each according to a set government standard applicable to all things, including money, cars, sex, entertainment—to each according to a set government standard applicable to all. Gore tried to convince voters that with enough money the government could do anything, including induce aliens to visit earth. In contrast, we in J3's campaign believed that if the government did nothing, it would improve.

As the campaign rolled toward November 2000, we struck out into the hinterlands to brainwash the electorate. A "Perfect President" was a high standard even for J3 so we had to roll him and public opinion into a symphonic match. And we had to prepare for the presidential debates—where everything, we hoped, would come together.

EMTs, researchers, volunteers, and consultants blossomed like broccoli on a campaign dinner plate. Sarah set aside a whole wing for me on Money Street—with a corner office, secretaries, and personal assistants. I soon wore Brooks Brothers suits, and the staff called me Mr. Smith more often than Smitty. I gazed down on M Street at the homeless I knew so well. I considered walking down to see them again—or bringing them up to see me. But we inhabited different worlds now.

The polls predicted that the election would run to the finish line: Gore held his own. Despite the Monica episode, Clinton's popularity bled over to his VP. I crossed paths with Gore a few times and liked him—he paid attention when I spoke. He asked once about Mr. Surlepont's death, but I referred him to Big Tits. Flack-Jack MacDonald insisted Gore liked to drink and party more than study his debate material.

Our EMTs prepared J3's briefing books with spicy unorthodoxies—Nazis in New Zealand, gays in Ghana, mangos in Murmansk. They cited experts, asked off-the-wall questions, and pasted uncut statements over traditional responses. When they finished, we had a quirky tome four inches thick with areas of interest for everyone on the planet except the voters.

And possibly the DC homeless who passed right beneath my window. How could I, a compassionate conservative, ignore a segment suffering from financial oppression, mental illness, and drug and alcohol dependence, especially when the unchosen had flung J3 so prominently into the news? With the addition of another staffer—one like Leroy Stivers, connected to the local street-power structure and even the City Council—I might add perspective to the campaign. The homeless disregarded convention—so, I thought, Leroy might see things others miss. While ruminating, I saw Leroy lugging his grocery cart down Money Street. Before he got away, I sent Flack-Jack MacDonald down to grab him. Full cart and all, Leroy wheeled into my office. He couldn't believe his eyes when he saw me. "I heard you were important—but man, this is something!"

"Do you want a job? I can give you good pay, health insurance. You could afford an apartment."

"Are you putting me on, man? What would I do?" He hesitated. "I would embarrass you."

"Leroy, it's still me. You'll do fine. You won't embarrass me any worse than the Presidential Suite—and look how good that turned out. It would be fun to have you."

"Still searching for a conscience, Smitty?"

I laughed. "I saw you and started thinking how valuable you might be to the campaign. You're my best friend. It's a Republican thing—friends helping friends."

"What would I do?"

"Make copies, run errands, help me—watch my back. You can write speeches; you could tell J3 a few things. Look, man, I'm trying to use your bad-ass, useless talent."

"I can't read very well."

"You can too. You were a sergeant and cop for Christ's sake."

"I mean, I can't see small letters anymore. I need reading glasses."

"Oh. Here, take J3's reading glasses." Leroy smiled a big I-also-need-a-dentist grin. I gave Leroy money for clothes and sent him with Jack-Flack to Wal-Mart. This little bit of do-gooding left me in high spirits—until a few days later when Leroy showed up in ruined clothes. "I had to sleep in them," he explained.

I should have known. "OK," I said, "you'll live with me until we figure this out."

"What about Buster Keaton?"

"What do you mean?" Was Buster Keaton, my quiet Heinz 57 mutt, still alive? I loved that dog, but now I was instantly afraid that a new attachment would leave me even more grief-stricken if something happened. My fear of commitment had kept me from buying him a collar, a license, and keeping him close—and later I felt responsible for his fate.

"Buster Keaton is back, man. He wandered down Kansas Avenue with a collar. He sleeps with me now. I feed him my own food so he won't take off again."

"Bring him to my place."

When Leroy arrived in a cab stuffed with his belongings, Buster Keaton's sad eyes scanned me ten times, flashed a gleam of recognition, and then—I swear—lit up in thirty-five colors that carried over to a huge, toothy grin. I hugged that mangy mutt and wrestled him to the ground while he gnawed on my arm and licked my face. The local vet gave our prodigal dog shots, declared him fit, and ventured that some munchkin was worried about him. None of us could have been happier, and Buster dogged Leroy and me every minute. I bought him a license, walked him every morning and evening—and then, despite my reluctance, put up posters on Kansas Avenue. I did have the slightest conscience. It was scary.

Leroy also needed medical care. His bad skin, teeth, and feet—from unwashed clothes, lack of hygiene and worn-out shoes—had wrecked a healthy body. But he was lucky; the Georgetown doctors could fix most of him. The homeless in DC suffered from infections, lice, hepatitis, endocarditis, and pulmonary embolisms. If you compounded their problems with alcoholism, drug abuse, and mental illness, they were lucky to live past forty.

It took more than a few weeks to straighten Leroy out, just as it had taken Sarah more than a few weeks to straighten me out. Leroy quit drinking, began to shower regularly, and even brushed his teeth. His DC Council member daughter invited him to dinner on a regular basis.

At first, Leroy felt uncomfortable in the world of work, but he oiled his rusty military and police skills. I gave him personal assignments: checking up on the EMTs or locating Liz or Sarah. In due course he fell into the rhythm, took and gave orders, cooperated in the campaign, and gave the EMTs his opinions. He appeared in campaign videos explaining the compassion of J3. Before long the doormen at the April Showers Hotel greeted him as Mr. Stivers.

As the first presidential debate in Boston drew near, I put Leroy to work copying and collating documents for J3's briefing books. The organization of the books was important, and we exploited Gore's stolen comments to structure it. On the first page of a section, we stated a question, such as, "What do you think of ferrets as house pets?" On the next page, we inserted the suggested answer: "I think the government should keep its nose out of the ferret business." On the following pages, we provided alternative answers in descending order of preference: "Everyone should own a ferret"; "Ferrets need love, too." On the final page, we inserted Gore's expected answers: "Ferrets need government-paid health care." We logged the order of preference of each answer by a rating system: 10 for the highest, then 9, 8, 7, and so forth. Once we finished with J3's master briefing books, we planned to duplicate the books for the staff.

I didn't convey the importance of the preferences to Leroy very well except to mumble, "Be sure to put all of the pages in their right order." In general, Leroy performed OK. He made the copies and punched all the holes. But he inverted the follow-on pages of suggested answers—placing them, with practical logic, first numbers first: 1, 2, 3, 4. So, instead of J3's reviewing the preferred responses first, he reviewed them last—or not at all. Providing health care to ferrets became our campaign priority.

This mistake didn't pop its ugly head until the debate. I'd flown to Boston with Liz and found seats in the third row of the auditorium at Boston College. Sarah remained backstage with J3 and his wife. Jim Lehrer, the moderator, instructed us at least fifty times not to react audibly, so we all tried to remain mute. But just as we went live, someone in the audience let out the loudest fart I'd ever heard, and the debates began on an ominous note—or notes. At first I thought the sound was a fire siren; but when a couple hundred faces aimed their chuckles at the offender, I realized that a Gore supporter had eaten too many Boston beans for dinner.

As Gore stepped onstage, he flashed a smile not unlike Leroy's. Far from appearing wooden, he projected warmth even to the Republicans. J3's entrance seemed less warm, but he possessed an unmistakable aura of confidence.

After opening remarks that restored a seriousness broken by the Boston beans, Lehrer directed his first question to Gore: "Could you please explain the comment you recently made about the inexperience of James Jefferson Jones?" Gore weaseled out of the answer by referring to J3's positions—not him personally. Gore then highlighted the prosperity enjoyed by all Americans. "We have the biggest budget surplus ever!"

J3 responded slowly—this was his first time since the convention in front of the entire nation on a live feed. "There is a surplus. We need to use the surplus; it belongs to the American people. We should use it to bolster the social security fund and provide more generously to the poor, especially to take the homeless off the streets. This would reduce crime. We should provide medicine to the elderly because the drug companies are making too much at the expense of the weakest segment of the economy."

Lehrer stared at J3. J3 had just given Gore's answer, the Democrats' answer. "Are you saying, Mr. Jones, that your Republican administration will focus on poverty programs?"

"Well, Jim, Republicans are people, too, and they lose their jobs, get old and sick. From the experience of my own staff, homeless people will become Republicans if they are healthy and have a place to live and vote. Sometimes the government should reinforce personal responsibility."

Lehrer stared at a baffled Gore. "Well," Gore began, "I guess I agree with Mr. Jones. We should help the poor and elderly and sick. But we have to show fiscal restraint. Mr. Jones uses fuzzy math when he tries to apply the surplus to solve the problems of the poor and elderly."

J3 cut in. "Fuzzy math? We have trillions of dollars of surplus. It would only take one to solve our social problems. You're the bozo using fuzzy math."

Lehrer cut in. "Next question for you, Mr. Jones. How do we reach oil independence? Should we open up the Alaskan wilderness to oil exploration?"

J3 laughed like Reagan. "Alaska is already open—I was up there campaigning, and no one stopped me at the border. The problem with oil is that we use too much to manufacture nuts and bolts. I drive an SUV gas guzzler that drinks more than my campaign staff. I own a home that pumps more heat than the women on 14th Street. I fish from a boat that consumes more liquid than it sits on. There are a million ways to cut down on oil dependence. First, we can develop more cost-effective manufacturing methods, drive more efficient cars, boats, and planes—and use alternative fuels like ethanol or hydrogen or even peanut butter. We can recycle old bikes and other junk we keep in the garage."

Both Liz and I groaned. J3 was repeating word for word the wrong answers—Gore's answers. J3 was supposed to say we needed to increase the production of oil, to open up the Alaska wilderness. Lehrer picked up on this. So did Gore: "It sounds like Mr. Jones is finally saying what we Democrats have been saying for decades. We need to cut consumption."

"Sure," said J3, "but we also need to increase production by innovating—not by pandering to the Mideast sheiks."

Lehrer interrupted. "Since you raised the point, Mr. Jones, I'll ask Mr. Gore the next question. How would you bring stability to the Mideast?"

Gore bubbled his answer. "With diplomacy. There's too much uncertainty. We need to work with our allies and the United Nations to obtain peace."

J3 looked even more confident. "The UN? When did the UN do anything to stabilize a hot spot? UN troops pull out when trouble comes. Look at the massacres UN troops allowed in Bosnia and Rwanda. If the UN can't stand up to a bad situation, who's left to protect the innocent? We need strident democracy.

We need to knock off dictators like Milosevic and Saddam Hussein and shoot the terrorists that oppose democracy."

J3 had again given the worst suggested answer in the briefing book, and I watched the Gore FARM Team descend on him. Lehrer responded before Gore could begin firing. "Are you serious?" Lehrer asked incredulously. "Assassination?"

"Why not? It would save us from future wars. It would save lives and cost less than a war. Even Pat Robertson, a man of the cloth, supports this approach. Look, Jim, if we're going to mess with maniacs, we need to take an aggressive stand—we have to fight fire with fire. We need to stop the little turds that wage covert war against the U.S.!"

"That's irresponsible!" Gore protested. "It's a violation of international law!"

"The Clinton Administration has refused to preempt the ruthless thugs in Iraq, Iran, and North Korea or that guy running around Afghanistan—Sam Laden. These people are evil, evil, evil; only by destroying them will their regimes change."

"You want to attack them before they attack you?"

"Why not? Why suffer American dead just to prove these clowns are going to attack us? We all know they're going to do something hostile. They hate America and want to kill us."

"You're a war monger!" Gore shouted.

"No, I'm a peace monger! It's better to sip the poison of a small skirmish than take a gulp of a global war. You were asleep at the switch when terrorism took over. Look at the bombing of the World Trade Center in 1993 by those terrorists. We're lucky the whole building didn't collapse and kill thousands. These bastards will try again. We need to kill them before they do."

"You're trying to scare the American people," Gore continued.

"You're crazy," J3 countered.

"You're an ass!"

"Fuck you!" J3 responded in a full blown bout of Tourette's that ended with about six *mf's*. At that, Gore left his podium and took a swing at J3—but J3 ducked. Security jumped onto the stage.

Lehrer attempted to calm the situation. "We'll take a ten-minute break." The television networks went to commercials—and one aroused commentator replayed Gore's swing until some boxer in Idaho called and told him that Gore threw leftist hooks. The chaos in the auditorium slowly subsided, but still no one knew what to do—although everyone hoped that Gore and J3 would apologize to one another so the debate could continue. Lehrer finally managed the situation with a statement: "This is the first time in history this has happened. We can terminate the debate right now or the two of you can control yourselves. What will it be?"

J3 pushed to resume the debate, but Gore seethed. Gore realized that he had lost it publicly—and that he may have lost the election. He had to scramble. "Let's go on," Gore whispered. When the debate continued, things only worsened for him. "I apologize for my actions," he stated as the cameras panned to him. "It was wrong. I hope you accept my apology, Mr. President." Mr. President? A Freudian slip?

"Of course," J3 replied diplomatically. "I just hope you wouldn't try that if you were president. It's one thing to use words, but another to overreact. You could start a war."

Gore tried to smile. "I thought you liked force, Mr. Jones."

"Used rationally."

"You think I'm irrational?" Gore asked.

"We'll let the American people decide."

Lehrer feebly cut short the exchange. "Let's move on, Mr. Gore. What's your stand on abortion rights?"

"Jim, I'm glad you asked. Every woman has the right to choose. I'm pro-choice and I believe that a woman has the right to control her body." Gore went on for a while until someone in the audience broke the rules and let out an audible snore.

When J3 finally answered, it became clear that he again had memorized the wrong section of the book. "I believe that all women have the right to choose. But women should choose life—not abortion. I wouldn't upset *Roe v. Wade*—but I would encourage adoption and the use of birth control rather than abortion."

Liz stared at me. "Is he OK?" she whispered. "He gave the Democratic response again."

"I think Leroy put the answers in backward in the briefing book," I tried to explain.

"If so, he's a genius. He just won the women's vote."

The debate actually finished, but in the end Gore looked like a homicidal maniac while J3 spanned the political spectrum from far bizarre to extreme mean. It was perfect.

XVII

Shortly after the fiasco, I took a gander at J3's briefing book. Yes indeed, Leroy had flipped the pages. Damage control symposiums awaited us, but I didn't worry as much that J3 had exposed his Tourette's syndrome to the world as I looked forward to slamming Gore for his temper. Leroy's mistake had transformed the campaign from a routine dirty-tricks contest into one that even Dick Nixon would have admired.

Two days after the presidential debate, Beelzebob debated SlowJoe Lieberman in Kentucky for the VP slot. No one watched except Idaho surgeon Fritz Wachenkopf, who was searching for emergency anesthesia for a gallstone patient. Unfortunately, Robby and Lieberman droned on long enough to knock out both Dr. Wachenkopf and his patient. The nation had become so intoxicated on Gore-J3 combat that their antics preempted the football season and all other entertainment. Broadway shows closed for lack of audiences. Had the electorate watched Fenster, at least, they would have learned that the JC PC's now connected Baton Rouge, Biafra, Bangladesh, and Brazil through satellite Internet.

We discouraged real issues and asked the voters to forget mundane things like Clinton and Monica and terrorism—and to split their sympathies between shouting "Fuck you!" and physically attacking your debating partner. We decided to make the election simple: FU was all right; going berserk wasn't.

The morning after the Robby-SlowJoe encounter, we cancelled the rest of the presidential debates, charging that Gore was a madman ready to unleash nuclear war if allowed in the White House. We conducted our own Money Street market research on the FU issue and concluded that the electorate saw the debates as prize fights. I felt that Gore really might deck J3 again for using the F-word.

Flack-Jack MacDonald accidentally initiated an internal debate by sending an email that said, "J3 infuriates people. He believes he's a genius and a visionary—but everyone else is an idiot." The email circulated to J3 himself. J3 called MacDonald, Sarah, Ron Durondon, me, and a few EMTs to his conference room. After apologizing to MacDonald for appearing so perfect, J3 fired him. "Fuck you!" MacDonald shouted on the way out. We learned a short time later that MacDonald was a double agent for Gore, and had stolen our position papers, including J3's inverted debate book.

After young MacDonald returned to the Gore FARM, I articulated our new tack. "The question isn't whether it's better to swear at someone or to smack them, but how to make FU appropriate to the American people. Everyone here can take the word 'fuck' and ignore its sexual meaning. We're going to use it is as a simple curse—like 'damn you' or 'go to hell.'"

Sarah looked at J3. "Is that how you used it?"

"I used it to say, 'Gore, I'm not going to listen to your crap.'"

One of the female EMTs replayed the episode on the conference room video. "Mr. Jones accused Gore of being crazy. Gore called Mr. Jones an ass, and then Mr. Jones responded with, 'F you.'"

J3 retorted with another episode. "I didn't say, 'F you'; I said, '*Fuck you!*' You have to be willing to say, 'fuck!' Fuck, fuck, fuck—*Fuck you!* Let's all say it together!"

We all mumbled together until FU began to sound like "Row, row, row your boat"—only with "Fuck, fuck, fuuuuuck you, fuuuuuuck you…" It was pretty ridiculous, but it seemed to work.

Still, Sarah promptly disregarded the order to say the F-word and instead turned to the head of the pollster section of the EMTs. "How have the American people reacted to FU?"

A little EMT stood up. "According to our poll, 42.5% of the American people admit they use FU at least once a week in their lives. But an amazing 85.3% have told someone FU at least once in their lives."

I watched the response. It was sinking in.

"Now, we also asked people how many times they called someone an ass, and the frequency was even higher. People feel that calling someone an ass is OK. But here's the kicker—only 32.3 % of the American people have actually taken a swing at someone when angry."

J3 looked baffled, but I understood immediately and spoke up. "So our strategy is to point out that J3's 'Fuck you!' was justified because it's a peaceful way of disagreeing. And it doesn't necessarily lead to smashing someone."

Durondon, who somehow reminded me of Dick Cheney, glared with the most incredulous expression. "You're going to tell the American people that FU is OK? Are you as batty as Gore? Anyone who says that is immoral."

"Not if the alternative is worse," I countered. "Look, the American people accept FU as a standard. They just don't admit it openly. Have you ever said it to anyone?"

Durondon shook his head. "Never. I've never said it—it's vile."

"I disagree," I argued passionately. "Have you ever defended yourself against a bully without resort to fighting? I'm sure you did, but I bet you've forgotten the FU you used. FU is like a growling dog—it's just a warning."

The debate lingered until J3 agreed to new political ads. One ad would show ordinary people saying "Fuck you!" when provoked. The second would show Gore losing his temper, with his middle finger on the nuclear button and Kim Jong Il exclaiming in broken English, "Fruck you!" We would pose the question, "Would you trust Gore to protect you?" Then we would produce a few ads with J3 giving a university lecture on the etymology of FU.

We made a party of the ads. Comedian Jay Leno asked our actors—Sarah, Liz, Leroy, guys on Kansas Avenue and Money Street disguised with mustaches, wigs and glasses—"Have you ever said FU to anyone?" When the actors hemmed and hawed, Leno said, "Come on—if I said you were an ass, what would you say?" At that point each one would say something like "Freaking you!" or "Famboozle you!" or just plain old "Fuck you!" Mouthing the four-letter word so much made it powerless. We needed an exclamation point just to provide some energy.

The instruction on etymology went just as well. We convinced one of the Georgetown linguistics professors to let J3 give a guest lecture. When J3 showed up in a bow tie and tweed sports coat with patches on his elbow, a packed house and cameras awaited him. He read a script: "The word 'fuck' comes from England as an abbreviation for a crime: 'For unlawful carnal knowledge.' Because of the Victorian attitudes in the latter part of the nineteenth century, sex remained hidden, and fornicating was strictly limited to marriages and an occasional brothel. If it occurred in the public eye, the magistrates found themselves at a loss for words. The crime of illegal fornication became unlawful 'carnal knowledge'—'carnal' meaning, by the way, 'meat' or 'flesh'—like 'carnivorous.' So illegal knowledge of meat was a euphemism for a terrible crime: having sex."

At this point, J3 stopped and looked up. "I wonder," he asked rhetorically, "whether it was illegal for women to consort with a salami?"

The kids hooted. J3 returned to his script. "When indictments came down for this crime of consorting with the wrong kind of meat, the English bills announced, "For Unlawful Carnal Knowledge." This also became too much to acknowledge and evolved into the initials 'F.U.C.K.' Finally, the abbreviation turned into a verb as in 'The bloke was charged with FUCKing."

After the cheers stopped, J3 took questions, which mostly consisted of students suggesting alternative theories or accusing J3 of exploiting the university. The *Washington Post* covered the event, and J3 appeared on the front page with the headline, "J3 Lectures on 'Meat.'"

The election had reached a dead heat when the meat ads appeared, but their radical departure from the feel-good approach of negative political persuasion pushed our positions in the polls. The Democrats ran their own ads, but they tried lamely to focus on the issues. Voters wanted to see J3 and Gore beat the hell out of each other. For the remainder of the campaign, I ran around with one big book filled with supporters of FU and a little one against.

Meanwhile, back at the ranch, Leroy moved into his own place. I kept Buster Keaton. Liz visited often but never remained long. She and Buster hit it off, and when she wasn't walking him, he crawled up next to her and slept. When I traveled, Leroy took care of Buster.

Considering our backgrounds, Liz and I did OK—she always wore jeans and a sweatshirt and I always wore a Brooks Brothers blazer and penny loafers. I cut way down on my visits with Sarah, who seemed content to spend her extra time with J3 or looking for a dress for the Inauguration.

J3's private life became public despite our best efforts to spin it as perfect. Linda didn't hang around J3 as much as Sarah did, and people began to talk. One evening on a campaign flight to San Francisco, Linda confessed her distress: "Jimmy Jeff doesn't want to sleep with me."

"He's working hard," I covered for him. "It's the strain of the campaign."

Linda's age certainly hadn't diminished her attractiveness, so I wasn't sure why J3 ignored her. She was from Biloxi, down to earth and resistant to most of the humiliation her husband heaped on her. She possessed that steel magnolia and Kevlar character modern Mississippi women claimed—and would make a fine first lady if J3 didn't use her as his rug.

"I understand you and Liz Fenster have developed a relationship. You make a great couple. But I don't understand Sarah and Paul Rivers. Sarah seems to ignore Paul. I think she, along with every twenty-five-year-old girl in Washington, is having an affair with Jimmy Jeff."

I faked surprise. "I don't think J3 would do it," I lied, "and I don't believe Sarah ever would either. She loves Paul. I've never detected anything to discredit her character."

"That's because she sleeps with you, too," Linda laughed. "Well, I caught Sarah in bed with Jimmy Jeff. How's that for proof?"

"You caught them?"

"Yes. She was right down on him, if you know what I mean. I've caught him with more than a few of those young women."

"This is more than I want to know."

"I never say anything. I don't want a scandal. I'll be a first lady if I don't divorce the son of a bitch. I just wanted you to hear it from me. Stick with Liz—she would make a fine bride."

When we arrived in San Francisco, Linda invited me to her suite—and of course I went. "I shouldn't have told you what I did on the plane," she said. "I hope you keep this hush-hush—even from Sarah." Linda looked at me in the oddest way; she had that "come hither" look Clinton boasted about when denying he had sex with Monica. "Can I ask you something?"

"Sure," I answered.

"Do you think I'm attractive? Would you sleep with me if you could?"

"Hypothetically speaking?"

"Yes, hypothetically."

"I would," I replied. "I'm sure all men find you attractive."

"Then why doesn't Jimmy Jeff?"

"He does. Men just have a tendency to wander."

"If I wanted a man to wander in my direction, how would I go about doing it? Should I go out to a bar, or should I invite him to my room?"

"I don't know." I didn't like where the conversation was heading.

"Well, suppose I invited a man here. What would I say to him?"

"I don't know, Linda. If he was the pizza delivery guy, you'd probably ask him how much you owed."

"Suppose I asked him to wait while I changed clothes. Would he wait?"

"For a tip, maybe."

Linda disappeared into one of the rooms of the suite and then returned in a few minutes in a red-and-black silk robe. "Do you like it?"

"It's very pretty."

"There's a robe in the bathroom for you, too, if you want it."

Here was the decisive moment. Linda knew I had a serious relationship with Liz—and she knew I'd been involved with Sarah. She was testing me. Linda just needed a man—any man—to confirm she was attractive. Why was I always the village idiot everyone used for stuff like this? Where was Mr. Surlepont when we needed him? "I'm not sure I can do this," I protested about as meekly as I could.

"Sure you can. You would do me a favor I could never repay. We all have secrets." Linda poured wine for herself as I sat thinking. What good could possibly come out of this? "Smitty, tell me what you think 'Fuck you!' means."

I coughed and nearly spit out my wine. "Well, we had a whole conference on that."

"So I heard." She smiled seductively. "Or better yet, what do you think 'Fuck me' means?"

This was too much for my incredibly weak resistance. I knew if I lingered a minute more I would lunge over the couch, grab her, untie her silk robe, and have the kind of sex only a desperate almost-first housewife could deliver—full of alienation and hunger. Fortunately, I managed to slink out of the suite with an excuse that Buster Keaton had eaten my campaign notes and I needed to refabricate them.

When I flew back east, I realized I almost had closed a circle of debauchery: I slept with Sarah, Sarah slept with J3, J3 slept with Linda and, but for Buster Keaton, Linda would have slept with me. So much for the moral strength of the GOP.

XVIII

The manipulation by our campaign intrigued me, especially the way we exploited gullibility to make people do things. When I lived on the streets, I lied and nothing much happened because everyone *expected* dishonesty. But when I lied as a high campaign official, people jumped. It was weird—but fun. I understood why power was so intoxicating: it was a form of entertainment.

Campaigning also was like running a machine. Add a little opinion here, twist an arm there, fly to San Francisco and flirt with Linda Jones, buy some loyalty, kiss a baby, kiss some ass—and the gears meshed. Wordsmiths controlled the levers because words supplied the raw material.

I became so impressed with the power of our EMTs, I changed my name to Jason *W.* Smith—the W stood for "Word." When I used my new middle name for the first time, my secretary corrected it to "Ward." I was now Jason Ward Smith. But I needed a Roman numeral to add real class: Jason Ward Smith *IV*. I figured IV was better than II or III. I never met I, II or III, but that didn't prevent me from inventing them as well. Jason Ward Smith I became a gambler; II a businessman; III a tycoon like Mr. Bobs.

The natural alliance of wordsmiths, pols, and pollsters evolved into a science. What regular people actually needed or wanted no longer mattered—only how we stage-managed events to take advantage of them. We were real about our surrealism. Democrats spun the electorate too, but idealism interfered with their ideology. Gore genuinely believed his own propaganda and injected idiotic ideas that detracted from his winning.

For example, Gore talked about "issues" in the abstract: "Why don't the Jones people focus on the 'issues'?" I sent a J3 letter to the Gore campaign and asked what "issues" he meant. Gore responded with a diatribe on worldwide hunger and health and predicted we would be wearing swastikas with our extremism.

I told Gore he should pay more attention to the local homeless if he had a real interest in hunger. Not only food, but life on the Washington streets was unhealthy—and a lot of Americans hovered nearer to the unchosen than any liberal wanted to admit. Sometimes only a few dollars and the smallest amount of food and security kept the underclasses functioning at all. I explained that the homeless often feared attacks—so some did paint talismans like swastikas on their clothes—but they still shared their food with one another, even when they had little. Show me a liberal, I demanded, who ever gave up his last piece of quiche to a hungry homeless person.

Gore liberals couldn't see the misery of the homeless at all. To admit something was to do something. Chosen liberals, of course, wanted to know about the unchosen in an abstract way—because liberals wore guilt instead of American flags on their polo shirts and lobbed the government at a social problem. But the unchosen remained completely unseen to most of the bleeding hearts—even if SUVs and Porsches pierced their blood-pumpers like an arrow from Cupid, or the IRS had them rushing for Limbaugh.

Gore hated our supporters—and called them special interests—although they were no weirder than his clique. But so what? The freedom to associate meant humanoids could come together to push for the restoration of the Confederacy or seek emancipation for plant life on Jupiter. In our case we called the humanoids Republicans, and we defined their interests as anti-government and pro-business—e.g., lower taxes, individual freedom and responsibility, national security. In Gore's case, we called them Democrats. Everyone belonged to a special interest: theater groups, ferret lovers, evangelists, gay scrabble players—you name it.

J3 had to persuade everyone—special interests or not—to see themselves in our positions. J3 had to become all things to all people. And that meant projecting more illusions. Our EMTs accomplished this in creative ways. We knew, for example, that much of the media didn't have their own reporters, so we supplied edited tapes for immediate airing. We even wrote their copy. We sent out panel commentators to bogus forums. We paid for everything—and we pulled in the free press. The free press remained free to disagree; but it was a business first, and we understood business better than the Democrats. We knew that reducing a radio station's expenses meant increasing its profits—and we knew that the free press jumped for anything free. To be free was to get something free.

We spun like spiders on speed. In fact, our EMTs, media consultants, and pollsters just plain lied to the special interests to win them over. But dishonesty worked. If we found a community that wanted to swim, we promised an Olympic-sized pool. If we needed the elderly to support the swimming pool—and J3—we promised free fitness programs.

Gore became apoplectic with our tactics because the Democrats didn't comprehend this new sort of freedom. I don't mean high school civics political freedom—but rather the liberty to flat-out lie. Once we decided that morals set up barriers to entry—to use economic terms—we made huge strides. The market worked: there was efficiency in deceit and fantasy worlds. The creepy part about busting moral restraints was that the religious right never recognized our tactics for what they were. Those folks spent way too much time selling souls rather than saving them.

Liz didn't like my approach and warned me that the campaign was going way too far. "Ends don't justify the means," she lectured me. "You're legitimizing corruption." She believed her brother had entered the race for pure ideals, but I had my doubts. Mr. Bobs already had earned a barge of bullion with the publicity from his JC PC and the increased value of his stock. Take away the technology and what did Fenster really have in the game? Within the rules of business, Beelzebob played it straight. But he could afford ethics. We in the campaign couldn't. They cost too much, and you couldn't eat ethics. Ethics in a presidential campaign was like a tank rolling over your toes—and we needed J3's to keep him running.

Despite my shabby exploitation of mendacity, Liz hammered away at the consequences of our recklessness. She explained the French Commune and the Rape of Nanking. She warned me about Nazi and Soviet propaganda—and argued that fear of outsiders led to genocides. She scared the hell out of me because she saw J3 unleashing totalitarianism in the U.S. "We have checks and balances to keep extremism at bay—but they don't work if the government sides with the extremists."

Liz wasn't street smart, but her moral sense inspired me despite my dissolute desires for J3. She told me about Plato's cave allegory. Prisoners stuck in a cave saw only shadows pumped in from outside—and believed they were real. One prisoner escaped, saw the authentic world, and came back to free the others. But they were so jaded they didn't believe the prisoner's version of reality, refused to leave and even tried to kill him.

Liz told me I was becoming the shadow maker—not the freed prisoner. I had escaped the street only to imprison the world—or to cast shadows with propaganda. I disagreed, of course, because J3 was inventing a better world for everyone. Sure, creating the better world required deception; but upon arrival in paradise, life would sparkle. Liz asked me to describe this great new world—and I came up short. "Everyone will have everything they want, and they won't have any enemies."

"Communism? Fascism?" she asked.

"Idealism," I said.

"You're no idealist."

True, but I was sure J3 was. Of course, that sent Liz off on a tangent by telling me that J3 had even fewer ideals than me. He was only constructing a "J3-ocracy"—a system that would hail *him*. I definitely disagreed. J3 didn't care what we made for him. He was just going all-out to become president. Political power wasn't his ideology. He was a narcissistic competitor, not an evil guy. He just wanted to win.

Liz invested a lot of emotional capital in me. Everyone liked me, she said—Fenster, J3, Sarah, Ron Durondon, General Hart, and even Bush. If we won the election, I would take a high position in the White House and assume serious responsibilities. Although Liz was trying to save me from myself—and maybe the country from a disaster—she pounded on me to accept that the world offered more than malice. The street suppressed beauty and love only because they were fragile. Their subtlety yielded strength if only I could see them.

XIX

The craziness of the campaign continued to a conclusion too close to call. The EMTs feverishly fabricated ads of Gore prepared to go postal. Gore's campaign retaliated with a video of J3 in the middle of a Tourette's tirade. Gore's FARM cultivated a hilarious production in which J3 swore like a sailor on fast-forward, unleashing more "fucks" than a Louisiana whorehouse.

Final projections showed that we needed every contested state to win.

On election eve, Liz and I, along with Leroy (who had become a star video actor), Robby Fenster, Sarah and Paul Rivers, General Hart and the Durondons, gravitated to J3's Georgetown home for dinner and an evening of voter results. The police provided security for miles; with reporters and neighbors nosing around, the scene outside became the freaky holiday of Simon and Garfunkel.

The night began with toasts to J3 and a thousand years of control. J3 and Leroy spent the meal discussing cheap ways to house the poor. J3 suggested that a brokerage firm administer a trust from the wages and social welfare payments of the underprivileged. Leroy proposed diverting foreign aid earmarked for Bumfuck, Egypt—"With money, the poor won't be poor." Ron Durondon objected to taking any cash from Egypt. "We need every penny to beat down those terrorists—even if we go broke doing it."

After dinner, the election results flowed as fast as the booze. Without warning, one of the networks projected Gore as the winner, and the house went into the sort of shock a meteor would cause if it landed in your lap. Linda Jones cried and left to lie down. J3 launched into a string of obscenities that turned the room blue—until he realized blue was the Democratic color. We heard cheers from Gore's tents at the Naval Observatory a couple miles away, which enhanced a sense of doom. Fortunately, no one really accepted that Gore had won. I sure didn't. Denial is a great thing. Sarah and I calculated and recalculated the electoral delegates as other results trickled in, and we concluded that the network projections were wrong. We had solid evidence that Florida supported us.

News channels joined the Gore bandwagon, thereby creating a sense of inevitability. After J3 settled down, he proposed conceding to show his graciousness. Beelzebob stopped him cold. "Look, *Jimmy*," Mr. Bobs said, "we've come too far to give up easily. Let's wait for Florida."

"You can't surrender until someone counts Dade and Palm Beach Counties—both Republican strongholds," Sarah added. "If the media is right, you can concede later. If it's wrong, you've given the election away. Look at all the people supporting you—all of our goals."

J3 seemed bewildered. "The press wants a statement. You make it, Smitty."

I walked outside where reporters lunged at me. "Smitty, what's going on? Is J3 going to concede?"

"We're looking at a deadlocked Florida. As Florida goes, so goes the election. It's too early to project Gore as the winner. We have to wait for all the votes, and this might take time. James Jefferson Jones, the next President of the United States, wants the American people to remain patient. We can be proud that America protects our right to vote."

I went back inside, phoned our Florida campaign chairman, Governor Jeb Bush, and asked what the hell was going on with the vote count. George W.'s brother explained: "The biggest Republican counties haven't come in yet."

"Well, get them in. If we don't win down there, you can be sure you and your brother will never see a national office except in a DC guidebook. You'll be poking around the Everglades as a tour boat operator, and your brother will own a mechanical bull in Texas." I paused to let my words sink in. "On the other hand, if you pull this off—and quick—J3 is ready to appoint W the UN Ambassador and you Secretary of the Interior."

Of course, I didn't have authority to promise anything of the sort to the Bush brothers; but what did I have to lose? I had a sneaking suspicion that Jeb Bush was sitting on the missing votes. I explained to Sarah what I'd done, and she only replied, "J3 already promised the UN post to a twenty-six-year-old bimbo working with the EMTs. But I'll talk to him."

This is how J3 changed history: a pile of Florida votes magically materialized, and J3 made off with the state and the election. Gore conceded in a terse statement to J3: "Fuck you, too." J3 walked out of his house to deliver his two-word victory speech: "We won!"

It soon sunk in to the world that J3 was going to become the President of the United States. Mr. Bobs would become the Vice President and Ron Durondon the Secretary of Defense and National Security Advisor. General Hart would take State, Sarah would head Health and Human Services, Leroy HUD, Jeb Bush Interior, George W. the UN, and Paul Rivers Justice. I was going to become the Chief of Staff to the President. The twenty-six-year-old bimbo would become the White House whore. It was a great day for J3, us, America, and the world.

XX

The high from winning took a few days to wear off: Republicans threw enough parties to change the drinking habits of the nation. Celebrations exacted their toll on J3, who had to appear everywhere, eat a plateful of food, and drink a shot of booze. Except for an occasional facial spasm and Tourette's outburst, he restrained his urges; but he didn't like the social interactions. He took off on vacation with Linda, four female attendants, three Secret Service agents, two turtle doves, and a partridge in a pear tree.

Liz and I flew to Aruba to celebrate the victory. This was my first time outside the U.S., and I saw why people picked the beaches: sunbathing stupid and lazy on the beach was a worthy goal. Although we explored the island in a four-wheeled jeep and nearly killed ourselves on the volcanic side, my head remained stuck to my cell phone. Calls from every single person I ever met in my life interrupted everything we did. People I never met asked for jobs and even cabinet positions. In order to slip out of a driving ticket, because the calls distracted me and I ran into a boulder, I conditionally appointed one of the local justices of the peace a Justice of the Supreme Court—if he decided to drop into Washington sometime.

Liz wind-surfed like a pro, but I kept falling off the board. When I finally gained forward motion I ran over some poor bastard swimming too close to me. I just wanted to sit on the sand, watch Liz, and pull strings via my cell phone. We—the royal we—had to reward the J3 sycophants and set up a transition team to deal with the transfer of power from the Clinton Administration. We also had to analyze a new Republican Congress and select issues for the electorate. Almost as many activists called to suggest legislation as supporters called to solicit jobs. Some of the more creative ones proposed projects compelling immigrants to undergo seminary training or requiring death row prisoners to become guided suicide missiles. I had my own legislative agenda; I wanted to brainwash the country with new ideas. What they were I wasn't yet sure, but new is new.

When Liz and I returned from Aruba, President Clinton invited J3, Mr. Bobs, General Hart, Ron Durondon, Bull Consep, and me to the White House for a security briefing. Al Gore, Louie Bluie (the White House coordinator for terrorism), and George Tenet, the current CIA Director, also dropped in. Clinton, to Gore's dismay, praised J3 for his fine job winning the election. "I couldn't have done it better—unless I brought in Franz Kafka to write my material." J3 took the reference as a compliment, but I took it as a sign that Clinton knew more than I gave him credit for.

Tenet and Bluie laid out the current terrorist threats on a computerized chart that filled an entire wall. Tenet noted that "We have porous borders, porous security in buildings, and porous politics. Anyone can infiltrate the country, poison our ideas, and do enormous damage."

Clinton added, "But this is the dilemma of America: either you keep the country open to preserve liberty, or you shut it down to preserve security. We've always chosen to leave America open. And this has great risks."

Ron Durondon shook his head. "With all due respect, Mr. President, America has refused to preempt terrorists—to nail them before they act."

"I'm a lawyer, Ron, and you can't convict a man for terrorism before he terrorizes. Remember that we have a presumption of innocence."

"I'm talking about war, Mr. President, not civil procedure. In war you don't convict an enemy soldier of being a soldier before shooting him. If he's a combatant—whether terrorist or otherwise—you kill him. Over the last eight years, the terrorists have committed horrible crimes against us."

Clinton smiled. "I guess we have a different philosophy. I always thought that you couldn't know an enemy *until* he does something to show it. Terrorists don't wear uniforms."

Gore added, "If we started shooting everyone who intended malice, we might have to shoot the entire Republican Party."

"You know what I mean," Durondon said.

J3 piped up. "I know what you mean, Ron. There's no point in arguing about whether we should start a war to root out terrorists. We'll deal with them in due course." J3 looked at me. "Smitty, you focus on this with Ron. You'll be the pre-White House coordinators on terror."

I didn't know anything about terrorism, but I read everything I could and made up the rest. I pumped Clinton's people, but even Louie Bluie, Clinton's guru, could tell me little because the FBI had yet to provide my security clearance. I pushed the FBI to complete its investigation; the gumshoes discovered quickly enough that I was only Jason Smith, homeless person, with a long record of petty scrapes with the law. They also ascertained that I had never attended Indiana University. In the end, no one cared, and the FBI spit out my clearance. J3 read my report and laughed when I admitted my real station in life and that I'd stolen his $20,000 bike. "You're a fine Republican," he said. "By the way, you can have the bike—it's just rusting in my garage. It still needs a new pedal."

We staffed up quickly enough, considering that I had no idea what I was doing. As Sarah concentrated on her duties as Secretary of HHS, I exerted control over the staff and delegated like a madman—and directed my delegates to delegate. I segmented a zillion governmental functions in some near-random order and engaged experts to fix my mistakes. I directed the transition team with the skill of a fly-swatter. I turned the EMTs into policy and speech writers and farmed out the inaugural festivities to Liz.

Just when I had everything under control, Linda Jones sought help for her role as first lady. Liz advised me to hire a manager for Linda so photogenic she would strike the press dumb and create an aura of glamour around the first lady. I called the hottest reporter I ever saw—a Wyoming TV rodeo cowgirl named Harriet Horsehead who announced the weather in painted-on jeans. Ready to heed the call of service to the nation, she arrived on Money Street in spurs, micro-skirt, and a ten-gallon hat. I convinced Linda that I'd spent hours reviewing Harriet's résumé, that the woman had great personal charm, could rope admirers for her, and could predict the rain to boot. Linda seemed more than thrilled with the outcome—and so did the barometric bronco-buster.

Leroy stuck around Money Street until the folks at HUD set up serious tasks for him. Leroy took his new life in stride. His daughter touted him in DC Council meetings for his dramatic rise to Secretary of HUD and his articulation of housing for the poor. Who knew better what a roof meant than someone who didn't have one? I vouched for Leroy with the FBI. He too had a healthy record of paltry thefts and drunkenness, but I figured (and apparently so did the FBI) this would qualify him just fine for government work.

Ron Durondon and I convened our committee on terrorism and enlisted Consep, Tenet, General Hart and future UN Ambassador George W. I added Ma Pucker, Louie Bluie and Zbigniew Brzezinski, President Carter's Secretary of State. Bush wanted to bring in some woman named Condoleezza Rice, but she lectured me as if I were the village idiot Linda craved in California, so I blocked her. I also invited Paul Rivers, Sarah's husband, because someone needed to explain the legal ramifications of wiretapping Americans, torturing terrorists, detaining suspects without a trial, and leaking secret agents to the press when it suited our political purposes. Tenet brought along a task force of experts. Of all the experts, I liked Bull Consep the best because he knew the major terrorists by their nicknames: "Killer," "Slayer," "Murderer," "Hit Man."

Opinions varied as to the definition of terrorism, with some parsing every sentence until they sentenced themselves to paralysis. As chairman, I restated what I heard—which was blah, blah, blah. One developing faction asserted that terrorism was just cheap politics and terrorists were a rag-tag army without uniforms. Ma Pucker argued that terrorists lined up with states for convenience. Durondon suggested, if that was so, that we separate the little bastards from their base of support in order to destroy them. The other faction, led by Consep, claimed that Islamic terrorism—which dominated current events—was rooted in a cultural reaction to western technology and secularism. Consep explained, "When only the Koran speaks God's will, only an infidel supports man's will. Since democracy is man's will, it clashes with God's." We all agreed on one point summarized by Durondon: "The goal of terrorism is extortion: to scare the shit out of people so they'll change their government's behavior."

"War is extortion," General Hart asserted. "It's always about forcing different behavior. Didn't we nuke the Japs and drop incendiaries on the Krauts to intimidate the civilians? Didn't we kill the buffalo—the food source of the Sioux Indians—to terrify their women and children? For Christ's sake, we killed 250,000 Filipinos—men, women and children—as part of the Spanish American War."

Durondon rolled his eyes. "Yeah, we killed lots of civilians—but all that was before the Nuremberg Principles. We killed civilians to stop killing civilians."

General Hart smirked. "It's OK if *we* kill civilians—but not the extremists?"

"We shouldn't have to kill civilians at all to advance our interests," Pucker tried to explain. "Western civilization relies on the just war concept."

Bush replied, "That's a Christian concept—no offense, Mama Pucker, but I think you're Jewish. As a Christian, it's never right to kill the innocent. That's why we're against abortion."

Durondon continued, "It's OK to kill civilians as a by-product of a battle. It's collateral damage."

I asked, "How do you distinguish civilians from combatants? Wasn't that our problem in Vietnam?"

"Look," Durondon stated, "the radical Muslims don't care if they kill civilians. We do. The purpose of terrorism isn't to fight fair, but to frighten. They can't frighten our military—so they frighten the civilians."

Brzezinski piped in. "If terrorists target our civilians, does that give *us* the moral right to target their civilians?"

At this point the committee agreed that the U.S. needed a tactic for targeting terrorists without unnecessary civilian damage. But the list of targets grew longer with each pet peeve—and the differences between terrorists and their populations grew less distinct. In order to reach consensus, we considered attacking Canada, France, Mexico, and China. General Hart shook his head. "We can't go to war all over the world. There are too many dictators and terrorists. We would never have the resources to carry it out. The American people won't permit it."

Durondon wanted to knock off the radical Muslims first. "Then we'll hit the leaders of the bad-guy countries—and the terrorist groups. We'll send in our spies and special forces."

"As the future UN Ambassador," Bush said, "I can assure you that the UN won't help."

"OK," I finally said, adjourning the conference. "I'll ask J3 what he wants to do."

J3 didn't want to do anything: "You handle it, Smitty. You know what to do."

I didn't. But Liz did. She advised me to limit our warlike activity. "The U.S. has too many potential enemies. You can't let the president assume he's above the law." Durondon and I proposed a plan that the committee accepted. But we kept it secret.

January 20, 2001, Inauguration Day, started off pretty well—although I didn't do much. Liz and I attended the swearing in and sat on folding chairs about twenty feet from J3 in front of the Capitol building. J3 gave a perfect speech about America returning to the land of the free, home of the brave, a place for opportunity, a place free of terrorism, and more blah, blah, blah. Sarah stayed by J3's side during the speech, irritating Linda so much that she returned by limousine to her bed in Georgetown until the next day when movers carried her and her bed into the White House.

Leroy attended all ten balls and chilled as a *nouveau* cabinet secretary. He had hired half the homies on the street as housing and security experts, and gave press interviews about proposed subsidized programs. I invited most of my street friends to the balls and arranged hotel rooms, tuxedos, and dresses for them. Carlos Rodriguez and Big Tits called me "Fairy Godfather"—because they knew that they would return to the shelters and heating grates.

Mr. Bobs threw a few lavish events—and gave away JC computers like breath mints. Liz and her brother danced a few times at the balls. Beelzebob thanked me in his gruff voice for fulfilling this dream. I thanked him for his beautiful and brilliant sister.

When Liz and I finally left the last party, I told her I had to report to the White House and that she shouldn't wait up for me. "I never wait up for you anyway," she said.

When I arrived at the White House, Durondon, Consep, and I descended to a situation room that dazzled us with high-tech displays, telephones, computers, video conferencing, satellite imaging—you name it. Clinton had spent a third-world treasury to track events. Reports from the field awaited us. The first was a mere warm-up for those that followed: "Jughead walks the line"—meaning that Yugoslavia dumped Milosevic. As Durondon deciphered the email, videos, and telephone data, I listened in awe. "Milosevic is seeking asylum in the Hague."

The first violent report came in via satellite telephone: "Garcia struck out."

"What the hell does that mean?" I asked Consep.

"It means we assassinated Castro."

"We killed Castro?" I asked.

"Correction: not 'we.' The anti-Castro forces in Cuba."

"Oh shit!" I shouted. "What's going to happen now?"

Durondon smiled. "Most likely the leadership in exile will invade."

We waited and drank coffee. It was now 3 AM. Another report came in by email. "Bob bought the farm."

"Bob?" I asked. "Not our Mr. Bobs, I hope."

"No, Robert Mugabe," said Consep. "He was destroying Zimbabwe and killing civilians."

Pretty soon another big one arrived: "It's not a sunny day in Baghdad."

Consep and Durondon gave one another high-fives. "We got the bastard!"

"Saddam Hussein?" I suspected.

"The whole Mideast will change."

Reports arrived at a steady pace: "UBL is DOA" and "Ben is banned."

Consep translated the first to mean that Usama bin Laden was dead. "He was the worst of all." Consep thought bin Laden was plotting to hijack planes and crash them into the White House. The second report meant that the Taliban in Afghanistan—the leadership that supported bin Laden—had been defeated.

"What else?"

In due course we learned that Yasser Arafat ate a hand grenade, Kim Jong Il bled to death from a penile aneurysm in a brothel, and a goat trampled Qaddafi of Libya. Lukashenko of Belarus suffered a heart attack from working out, and Mubarak of Egypt suffered a heart attack from not working out. The Saudi Royal Prince and important sheiks were killed on a flight to Las Vegas; nasty Asian leaders choked on their food; the leaders of Syria, Chechnya, Myanmar, Moldova, and Haiti disappeared on a Carnival Cruise. Out went the dictators of Sudan, Eritrea, Ethiopia, and Swaziland. The leaders of more terrorist organizations than I could identity vanished into thin air. And then a thick sheaf of documents came in.

"Oh, no!" Durondon exclaimed. "We've just knocked off all the Stans."

"Stans? Stan who?" I asked.

"Uzbekistan, Tajikistan, Kyrgyzstan, Turkmenistan, Waziristan, Kazakstan, Pakistan, Kurdistan. There are a couple other Stans thrown in, too."

"Are all of those countries? Isn't Pakistan our ally?"

"Oh, hell," Durondon said.

By 8 AM Washington time, on January 21, the world faced chaos. Populations started knocking off their leaders and terrorist organizers without any prompting from us. Revolts broke out—and some weren't good. In France, for example, the Bonapartists held the prime minister hostage. I called the new president and told him who we had assassinated. After reciting his standard Tourette's vocabulary, he put the military on the highest alert. The *Washington Post* screamed, "WORLD REVOLUTION!" on the front page and stuffed the news of the Inauguration on page 8 with the headline, "J3 Becomes 43," which I could now translate to mean that J3 had become the forty-third American president.

All we could do now is sit back and watch the show.

XXI

We didn't wait long—and international actors tap danced like Gregory Hines when it came. Accusations and counter-accusations grabbed the spotlight so selfishly that no one—not the New York, London, or Japan *Times*—knew how to describe this unconventional launch of a presidency. Either J3 had committed the most massive crime in history or he had triggered the most revolutionary change of any leader in history. But in any case, even the angriest statesmen had to agree that the "Inauguration Revolution" killed very few people. And when 99.9999999 percent of the population checked in on the first days of the J3 Administration, they learned about the relatively few bad apples that had checked out.

Still, the threat of war loomed everywhere; armies *and* terrorists wanted to march. But they didn't know where exactly *to* march; so they plotted their responses with the thoughtfulness of heated hyenas. Should they attack U.S. interests, kill Americans, ally with one another in one massive axis of evil? We feared they would devise something clever, but the leaderless terrorists needed time to shape a coherent plan. In the meantime, it became obvious to every man, woman, and child on earth that the U.S. had spoken. And the message was: "We don't like dictators and terrorists—especially ones who disagree with us." Apparently we didn't like international law either.

By the evening of January 24, world opinion divided into those for us and those against. We had shuffled the decks; the bad guys picked up deuces while we picked up the aces. South America remained stable—no problems there. *Fidelistas* accused Cuban exiles of Castro's assassination and tried to install his brother Raúl as president, but brother Raúl succumbed to a bribe by Cuban businessmen from Miami. Exiles landed with trillions in trinkets and cash in a more successful replay of the Bay of Pigs. The Cuban army, smelling the money, disbanded and opened restaurants, arcades and souvenir shops.

The armies of Libya and Syria took control of their countries. The generals in charge, however, announced that they had no quarrel with the U.S. and would attempt reforms. At U.S. urging, the World Bank and the IMF poured loans into the countries. The Shiites and Kurds in Iraq appealed successfully to the Sunni Baathists in power to form a new constitution. The neighboring Saudis faced their own upheavals, overthrew the royal family, and reformed along fundamentalist lines. But with threats from J3 about bombing holy sites, they agreed they would support the infidels within Muslim guidelines.

Iran grew a little irritated with us after many of its malevolent mullahs went down on a boat trip to Basra. But the Iranians weren't sure what exactly had caused their ship to sink. Although Consep had paid dissident Iranians to torpedo the tyrants, the Iranian people merely suspected the U.S. and held their reactions.

The Israelis and Palestinians developed a working relationship after fifty years of war. Terrorism and car bombings declined sharply. They still hated one another, but they realized that the world had grown tired of their bickering.

The Stans turned out less problematic than we'd expected. Afghanistan blamed the Northern Alliance for the assassinations, but when the ruling Taliban fell, a new self-determining regime arose. Eventually, democratically elected warlords regained their position in the world as the prime source of opium. Pakistan blamed India for its forced transformation and launched a brief nuclear war in Kashmir that killed a few million goats and sheep—and Chernobylized the area. In time, the two neighbors reached a peace treaty that stuck because Kashmir now was worthless and both sides had to address a refugee problem. The other Stans blamed Russia, despite clear and convincing evidence that we paid the assassins.

Fortunately, we hadn't tangled with Russia or China or Europe—so they couldn't do too much to us—even after they figured out what happened. The successors to Lukashenko in Belarus asked the countries in the EU to provide protection against Russia, but Putin reincorporated the region into a union in which Putin served as president for life.

The North Korean population remained in shock. But South Korea poured food and aid into the country and reunified without resistance from the North Korean army. Countries like Myanmar and Zimbabwe quietly reformed.

We lost only one undercover agent in all of the operations—a woman who accidentally asphyxiated herself when the four-hundred-pound asthmatic she was assassinating had an attack and fell on her. Bull Consep and Ron Durondon were positively gleeful at the cost-benefit ratio. They praised J3 for giving them a free hand.

It took about a week after the Inauguration Revolution for the intellectual community to pin the tail on any donkey. Miraculously, the majority of the tail-pinners joined the "for us" side. No one except Danish cartoonists and some islanders in the Pacific blamed the U.S. outright for any of the mess. One French writer asked, however, "Is it best to assassinate bad guys, start wars to rid the world of them, or leave them in place? Monsieur Clinton left them in place—but President Jones decided that preemptive attacks to rid the world of dictators and terrorists were the best choice for *liberté et égalité*. Doing nothing was the worst."

Secretary of State Hart had his work cut out explaining the U.S. position. He did OK—all things considered. We would support our allies in Europe and the rest of the world, but we would remain on the side of freedom—whatever that meant. To me, it meant we would support those countries that were "for us."

George W. was right about the UN—it was toothless. We also learned that it was corrupt. Saddam Hussein had paid off UN officials to sell its embargoed oil. This irritated J3 so much that he pulled out of the UN until it fired the old Secretary-General and established a standing army subject to executive control of the new Secretary-General. Ambassador Bush made an impassioned plea for honesty: "When I was a kid, I watched Superman on TV. He wanted truth, justice, and the American way. So today, I ask that that we stamp out graft in the UN and graft truth, justice, and the American way on the UN." Bush conveyed his ideas so well that the UN membership "for us" elected him the new Secretary-General, and the U.S. rejoined.

The weeks and months that followed the Inauguration Revolution brought new order to a new world. Under this, the president assumed "unitary executive" authority over the three branches of government—meaning J3 could override Congress and the courts in pursuit of declared or undeclared war, and democratic states could disrupt non-democratic states. International law changed drastically under the "J3-B3 Doctrine." It was OK to start preemptive wars and assassinate unsavory leaders. And in order to find terrorists, it was OK to kidnap and hold suspects without a warrant, lawyer, or trial, and to wiretap calls. Secret prisons expanded like Italian meals and they hit the eye of J3 like a big pizza pie with extra toppings of *amore*.

One night, after a potent Tourette's outburst hit a White House aid who forgot to escort J3's girl *du jour* to a late night briefing, J3 got the bright idea that if torture had flair, the rack had panache. J3 asked me to find out if we could torture his tormentors, starting with his negligent aid. J3's more rational desire was to use the rack—but not necessarily the pinion—if it also yielded useful information. I called Paul Rivers, the new attorney general, figuring that J3 couldn't openly use torture, let alone dust off the paraphernalia from the sixteenth century. "What does the law say?"

"The law says J3 can rack and roll terrorists to his heart's content."

"Are you serious? What about Americans who show up late with his daily meal?"

"Define them as terrorists, and you're good to go."

"Won't their lawyers claim the rack is cruel and unusual punishment—especially if we get caught?" If I had learned anything on Kansas Avenue, it was that the police couldn't beat you up in plain view of witnesses.

"They don't get lawyers. Besides, it's not cruel and unusual punishment if there's no trial. Punishment is post-trial."

"So we can torture people before trial to get information?"

"If the bad guys are terrorists," Paul explained, "they're enemy combatants. They don't get trials. So it's not punishment."

"Let me get this straight: First we classify them as terrorists. That way they're enemy combatants. If we capture them in the war on terror, they're prisoners of war, and we don't have to put them on trial. Without a trial, they never get the protections against cruel and unusual punishment because we aren't punishing them. Is that right?"

"You got it."

"What about the Geneva Convention?"

"It only applies to countries at war, not to illegal terrorist organizations or individuals."

"So we're free to torture terrorists for any reason?" I asked.

"Sure."

"Any sort of torture? The rack?"

"Anything you want—pulling out fingernails, *strappado*, electrodes."

"We're all going to hell."

At first the American people seemed skeptical—and restive. But in a propaganda blitz we extolled the virtues of torture, indefinite arrest, lack of representation, secret prisons, and warrantless wiretaps. We dug into the archives and found commie and Nazi films to spin the positive things cruelty did for the civilized world. We directed the EMTs to produce a film called "Saved by a Rack," which featured a dark, swarthy, unshaven terrorist about to party with his pals in paradise by blowing up the St. Louis subway system. Just before meeting up with them, the FBI wiretapped his cell phone. FBI agents dressed in white radiation-and-bacteria suits caught him, took him to a secret prison in the basement of a department store, and strapped him to an old-fashioned rack with lots of electrodes. When the good guys stretched him until his joints popped, he disgorged the details of the plot. Armed forces swooped in moments before the evil terrorists could blow themselves up. The EMTs made an exciting movie; I thought it might become a box office hit if we licensed it.

In press releases we pounded out our mantra: ends really did justify the means. If we couldn't stop terrorism peacefully, we would restrain it with any tool at our disposal. This was total limited war.

Despite overseeing the film production, I had my doubts about the effectiveness of torture, even on an emergency basis. When the police had harassed me on the streets, I told them whatever they wanted to hear. Why not? Usually they had some fixed idea anyway, so reinforcing it gave them what they wanted and let me continue life without a dented head. Ron Durondon assured me that torture worked pretty well. New drugs, taken once every three minutes, and psychological techniques like threatening to kill family members, extracted information in less than an hour if used effectively.

In any event, we rounded up all kinds of terrorists—from suicide bombers to newspaper letter writers—and found that good citizens willingly fingered every troublemaker in their midst. Since George W. now ran the UN and deputized local armies to ferret out terrorists, we cleansed the world of bad guys. To be sure, we netted a lot of innocents and tortured them, too. But they turned in their families and neighbors—and although we sometimes lost track of the real terrorists, we stopped a lot of crime. Ron Durondon set up a camp in Guantanamo, Cuba, for the toughest cookies. When I needed a break, Liz and I flew down to hang out on the beaches for a day or two.

Again and again, I thanked God that I was a sociopath so I didn't have to feel guilty about all the damage I was doing. I don't know how Bush and Durondon dealt with it.

J3 dealt with it by starting White House Television to control and sanitize the news. I assigned the EMTs to the operation, hired correspondents, and produced a channel for news the way we wanted it. Our motto became, "All the News We Want You to Have." We made tapes and interviews to describe the new freedoms the world now enjoyed. We screamed out the stories of global populations spontaneously leaping in the direction of democracy and freedom the day J3 became the Perfect President. Mao couldn't have done it better.

In one interview, J3 emphasized that freedom had a cost—and the cost was the freedom we used to have. His interviewer, Jim Lehrer, wanted to know how we gained more freedom from being less free. J3 told him we had to look at the quality of freedom. "We give up the freedom to terrorize in exchange for the freedom to obey the law."

"Are you saying that obeying the law is freedom?"

"Of course," J3 said. "Think of it as a secure environment. Inside the boundaries we do whatever we want as long as we don't disrupt things. We have jobs, family, religion, schools, businesses free from terrorism."

"Whose idea is this?"

"It's America's idea, capitalism's idea, democracy's idea. It's a perfect idea—trade useless freedoms like terrorism for secure freedoms."

On White House Television, we always ended up with a great interview, but Lehrer wanted to push the envelope. "Hasn't the Jones Administration conducted random searches and wiretaps among ordinary citizens? Don't we have to watch what we say and where we go? We're bombarded with phony news. What sort of freedom is this? *A Brave New World*?"

J3 thought for a moment. "Looking at freedom through the lens of the pre-Inauguration Revolution of course makes no sense. You have to understand freedom within limits. You live well within a television studio, or at home, or on vacation. But if I put you out on the street—where my Chief of Staff Jason Smith and my HUD Secretary Leroy Stivers lived—you wouldn't do well."

"It's all just the *type* of freedom?"

"Sure. We limit our environment—and therefore our relative freedoms. Terrorists aren't as free as us in an objective sense. They live hand-to-mouth, always underground or in some sneaky identity. They can't reveal themselves."

"So you're saying we're not so bad off—we're more secure than terrorists?"

"Our brand of security provides natural freedom—theirs provides paranoia. Jim, this is America. We come and go as we please, we criticize our presidents without fear of arrest. And we're free to fail. Failure makes for good business strategy: you avoid loss by maximizing your assets and minimizing liabilities."

After the interview, we noted a substantial rise in the polls for J3. We disrupted global terrorism. The politics of the planet settled into new dynamics that favored democracy—and for about eight months everything went very well. J3 looked flawless—wise, calm, popular. The stock market soared.

Vice President Bobs extended Money Street to the entire world; the business community clung to him like fruit flies to a giant mango. Pearless stock split so often people used the certificates for insulation. Robby-Bobby delivered on his gift of a computer to every high school graduate: the JC and the nano-JC dominated the market. You just slid the tiny computer into a monitor or a cell phone and punched in data on a wireless holographic keypad. With earphones and video glasses, you listened to infinite music and movies, conducted video conferences, retrieved White House News or lectures, or examined library books on the other side of the planet. This was real freedom.

Needless to say, we learned much in those first months. I discovered the importance of flooding forums with good old all-American propaganda—not the hokey rhetorical stuff that required a political dictionary. Plain stuff like, "We in America believe that honesty is the best policy—even when the hard truth is painful." Then, of course, we'd tell our citizens something other than the hard truth. The American people believed so much in the J3 government that as long as we looked sincere, they accepted whatever we fed them.

Ma Pucker called one day to complain that J3 looked like Hitler and Stalin. She kept saying that "the enemy at the gate" approach would backfire. Even if we hoodwinked the American people, we couldn't dupe the rest of the world. "Did you ever read Lincoln's quote about not fooling all the people all of the time?"

"Sure," I said. "But Presidential Directive 5432 has amended that. We're bringing peace and freedom to everyone—including fools."

"You must think we're all stupid, too."

Everything went well enough on the international level to let us pursue a few domestic issues. I invited Leroy to meet with J3 in the White House in preparation for a congressional appearance. "Well, Leroy," J3 asked, "what do you plan to say about HUD?"

"I intend to describe the new housing programs for the homeless. We're going to subsidize McMansions in the suburbs: big houses that have three acres of land, two-car garages, four or five bedrooms, maybe a pool."

"If this is a Republican program, I want to be out of town when you propose it."

Congress didn't like it. But because we controlled Congress, Leroy won support when he presented his proposal to the House Banking Committee. "Harrumph! Secretary Stivers!" one crusty good-old-boy congressman remarked on camera, "Your desire to help the poor is commendable. I will support your efforts to eliminate the poor by giving them more money. It's cheaper in the long run to buy them than to maintain them."

Leroy was on a roll—so he returned to Congress to propose nationalizing inner-city apartment buildings. "This way," he explained to the committee, "we can make a fair distribution of a scarce resource." Because there weren't many apartment buildings, Leroy asked for money to buy condo units. The Republican chairman of the committee objected, but Leroy called J3 who in turn convinced the committee that this add-on legislation made sense.

Although we worked together to advance humanity and certainly respected each other as collaborators, J3 and I never became close cronies. J3 didn't get close to anyone except Sarah and his harem. With Sarah often tied up in J3's office as the Secretary of Health and Human Services, J3 hid away in the White House bunker with his favorites. Linda Jones wasn't sure whether Sarah improved the situation or not, but I saw a trend: J3 spent more time loving his girls than loving the country. Still, peace broke out all over the world. J3's popularity skyrocketed as high as any president in history—an amazing 95% approved of him—and people compared him to Washington, Lincoln, and Roosevelt for his courage in knocking off tyrants and providing for the poor.

Linda stormed into my office one day and told me that she had had enough of J3's undeserved adulation and wanted to leave town. I trumped up a boondoggle for Brazil and made the first lady and Harriet Horsehead J3's emissaries. When they arrived in Rio on Air Force One, they made a beeline for the beaches. About 300 photographers captured them in thong bikinis with microtops, waving in the waves at the boys from Brazil. The *Washington Post* plastered one picture on the front page with the caption: "Working Hard in Rio." Linda sure had a nice backside for a forty-year-old, and Harriet had an incredible set of jugs. When they returned to the White House from their official duties, senators and congressmen chased them both like wayward calves.

I kept chasing Liz—and one day I finally tackled her in a football game, nearly broke her leg, and threatened that if she didn't marry me I wouldn't let her up. Robby-Bobby threw a large wedding for us on September 8, 2001, on the White House lawn. Liz looked, as everyone commented and expected, breathtakingly beautiful in white set against the red-and-blue flowers filling the entire lawn. Buster Keaton made his social debut by sharing with Leroy the role of best dawg. The President came—along with the cabinet, the congressional leadership, a few Supreme Court Justices, Carlos Rodriguez, Big Tits, and Amy. Ron Durondon told me that if I ever wanted a degree from Harvard, he would arrange it. I told him I first had to graduate from high school.

Sarah and I kissed one last passionate time before I took my vows. Carlos wandered the White House lawn eating and drinking until he puked in the

Rose Garden. It must have been a sight to behold—but since I was busy promising eternal love to Liz, I didn't get that pleasure.

J3 was very gracious and gave the first toast at the wedding reception. Intense security surrounded the affair. The mass of guests were actually Secret Service who declined to drink. J3 told all the guests that Liz was probably too good for me, but I had proved I had adequate *cajones* not only by taking on Liz, but by taking risks with him. J3 praised my help in bringing him into office and carrying out the Inauguration Revolution that changed the world.

I toasted Liz, J3, Mr. Bobs, Sarah, Leroy, and Buster Keaton for their faith in me.

Liz reminded me in her toast that a conscience evolved as a protective device. She pricked my sense of right and wrong throughout the evening as urges surfaced to let loose, drink too much, eat too much, say too much, and jump on her. But when the bedroom doors closed behind us, my conscience went sound to sleep just as my *feeling* woke up.

XXII

On the morning of September 11, 2001, I boarded a plane at Washington Dulles for a flight to LA. The trip messed up my honeymoon, and instead of beautiful Liz hanging on my arm, three Secret Service agents surrounded me—including J3's personal pug-faced bodyguard, Deuce Brucie, who intended to connect with the Wiz in California. As I found my seat in first class, I spotted three Arabs even uglier than Deuce sitting with an attractive woman across the aisle—all looking like they'd robbed a bank with their alert eyes cast down to avoid contact. The men must have robbed *someone* because, with their bad teeth, bad haircuts, and Wal-Mart clothes (evident from the tags still dangling from their shirts), I identified with them: they obviously didn't have enough money for Egg McMuffins, let alone first-class tickets.

The J3 Administration had mandated thorough security checks after the Inauguration Revolution; and Dulles Airport complied. I read a briefing paper, but the bad vibes shook me harder than a backward ride on an Ocean City roller coaster. As I looked up from my paper, the woman stared with a slight smile. This didn't seem natural because people in first class never smiled at anyone. As we taxied for takeoff, the woman suddenly became friendly toward me particularly and asked in a British accent if I was Jason Smith. I told her I was, and she introduced herself as Melissa El Karazi.

"Going to LA for business?" I inquired.

"Unless we fly somewhere else." Ms. El Karazi hesitated, then told me she was a computer salesperson taking her three ugly mugs to a training class. I asked if she was making much money. She said not yet, but she was try-ing—she had just started her business. I kicked Deuce because no self-respect-ing start-up entrepreneur would pay first-class fare for three Wal-Mart employees. Hell, Sarah didn't let me fly first class until J3 won the nomination.

Ms. El Karazi opened a magazine, but her hands shook so much she couldn't hold it. "Why wouldn't you fly coach to save money?" I asked.

"We were upgraded."

"Oh," I said. "What kind of computers do you sell?"

"Pearless computers. The new JCs. Everyone wants a JC."

"My brother in law is connected with Pearless," I said. "Do you have a card?"

"No, I don't have one."

Despite the prohibition against using a cell phone on a plane, Deuce Brucie contacted his office, and I called Liz. It turned out that Melissa El Karazi was an Egyptian student—and had come to the US to learn to fly. Pearless had no record of her. I whispered to Deuce, half in jest and half seriously, "I think this chick might be a hijacker."

Deuce took the serious half and asked Ms. El Karazi to stand up, which she did. Deuce searched her. She swore at him when he patted her butt, but that's where he found a box cutter. "I open computer boxes with it." We weren't sure what to do. The flight attendants seemed bewildered, and the other Arabs glared at us. When I felt threatened like this on the streets, I took action—smacking someone or taking off. We couldn't do either, but Deuce Brucie at least was armed with two guns. I asked the flight attendant to order the captain to taxi back to the gate.

She left to talk to the captain, and the plane pulled into a spot and stopped. The captain walked back to our seats and introduced himself to Deuce Brucie. "Why should we go back?" the captain, obviously pissed, asked so loudly that the people in coach complained.

Deuce Brucie wanted to keep things calm. "Because this man is the Chief of Staff to the President of the United States, and he needs to get out for national security purposes."

"We can't do that—we're ready to take off."

"Oh yes you can. I'm Special Agent Deuce Brucie of the Secret Service, and I'm ordering you to return to the gate."

I then asked the captain to lean down so I could talk to him privately. "There's a security threat on the plane." I nodded toward the Arabs.

The pig-headed captain let loose again with his booming voice. "You're a bigot. They thought Arabs blew up the building in Oklahoma City—but they were Americans. Who's going to pay for the fuel cost? I don't have the authority to taxi back."

"I'm giving you the authority," I said.

"Unless the company instructs me, I'm not changing anything—Chief of Staff or not. I'm the top guy on this flight and I'm telling you all to sit down and enjoy the ride."

Deuce Brucie had enough and shoved the captain up against the bulkhead. "Turn around now or I'll arrest you."

"All right, all right," the captain stated. But when he disappeared, the door to the cabin shut, and we found ourselves on a take-off roll. Brucie and the other two security men charged the door of the cabin, pried it open, and cocked their Glocks at the blockheaded captain and the first officer. "Turn around now!" they shouted.

"OK, OK," the captain replied, "but we have to take off to avoid a crash."

Once we were airborne, we slowly circled to an approach. Melissa El Karazi and the other Arabs sat nervously in their seats but, fortunately, did nothing except play with the tags on their clothes. When we landed, a SWAT team waited. Deuce Brucie arrested the pilots for disregarding his order and detained the Arabs for questioning. The captain was stupid for ignoring Brucie—and angry enough to quit his job on the spot. Because of the instant news coverage, the pilots' union walked out on strike, and every plane on the East Coast remained on the ground that day. But this had a positive effect.

The quick grilling and torture of the Arab men and Ms. El Karazi (who had to strip in front of a few pop-eyed male interrogators) uncovered a plot of twenty Muslim extremists about to hijack five more planes once they received word that she had succeeded. One of the men admitted that the other El Karazi teams, part of *al Qaeda*, intended to crash their planes into the World Trade Center, the Pentagon and the Capitol. Apparently Ms. El Karazi wanted us to drop in for a smashing tour of the White House. It turned out that she and the others were on a watch list the Immigration and Naturalization Service ignored. We learned the identity of all of the terrorists and hunted them down. "Look for first-class passengers wearing Wal-Mart clothes." Thank God I quit buying at Wal-Mart when I stumbled into Brooks Brothers.

We didn't tell the public much, but the media plastered reports of the pilot walk-out all over the news. I took flak for screwing up the air system for a few days, but fortunately no terrorist disasters occurred. Afterwards, we ordered better passenger screening, stronger cabin doors, and the elimination of box cutters, toenail clippers, and even metal knives with meals. We started questioning grandmothers and babies in case they had evil intentions.

J3 gave Deuce Brucie and his detail fifty awards for their courage and congratulated me for saving America. White House Television covered up the incident with new propaganda. Had I gone on to California, it reported, the taxpayers would have lost billions of dollars. The walk-out by the captain was silly, it said, considering the importance of the meeting that J3 himself had called (although he was waiting in LA for Deuce Brucie to deliver two young nymphs in coach). On the other hand, in order to ameliorate the upset to the system, we let everyone know that the Jones Administration had made flying safer.

J3 still looked more or less perfect.

The close call led me to think about Machiavelli—someone I admired for his amoral use of checks and balances. The world was filled with rotten people, but maybe other equally rotten people muffled them with quiet conflict. According to my dictionary, "Machiavellian" meant "unscrupulous, cunning, deceptive or dishonest"—or evil—but now I wasn't so sure. Smart political systems didn't stamp out evil. They countered it. If you pitted one evil against another—like Stalin against Hitler, or Iran against Iraq, or J. Edgar Hoover against Al Capone—you neutralized both. If you balanced evil forces, you channeled even their most obnoxious characters.

No one speculated about balancing the evil the hijackings could have unleashed. The potential results were too extreme even for the thinking of the EMTs. Maybe God and not Allah protected America that day. But maybe, just maybe, the injustices of the world cancelled each other. Maybe, after all—as radical as it might sound—the devil had a benign function: seeing and countering other evil. The chronic underexposure of Americans to danger left them unaware of the presence of real evil.

We at the White House knew of only two expensive and complex strategies to deal with the evil of terrorists: (1) physically contain the bad guys or (2) address the causes of bad-guyness. Neither recognized that evil could root out evil—that you could fight fire with fire if you didn't burn yourself in the process.

Suicide bombers posed the most difficult problems. We could contain terrorists for a time, but fanatics willing to die to kill innocents posed a challenge way beyond my abilities. The Israeli prime minister told me about a would-be suicide bomber—a kid of about fifteen—who had wrapped his family jewels in a wad of gauze surrounded by a steel cup. An Israeli soldier became wary when the bomber hobbled up to him holding the steel cup in place. The soldier stripped him right there and perused the paraphernalia: "Why are you so stupid? If you blow yourself up, your dick will land a mile away." The kid wanted to preserve his prick for the seventy-two virgins promised him in paradise.

Consep claimed that terrorism flourished when publicity killing became a cheaper way to speak than using your voice. Liz quoted Clausewitz who said that war was just another form of politics. If so, suicide bombing was also politics—an amoral form, to be sure, but politics just the same. To avoid terrorism, therefore, we had to make sure that all humans could express themselves peacefully and determine their own fate cheaply and without penalty.

Real self-determination was a daunting demand that had eluded even Woodrow Wilson, the inventor of the phrase. To me, effective self-determination required rapid change—and enforcement of human rights. J3 wasn't that ambitious. Rapid change to him meant a crusade—and crusades drained a treasury and evoked Western subjugation. You also needed to harness the will of the people to launch revolution. Americans weren't interested in war—or sending out assassination squads over and over again. They liked their lives as long as terrorists didn't blast them. They wanted to remain fat, dumb, and happy.

According to Liz, if the J3 Administration wanted to stop terrorism, we had to declare a *jihad* for free expression. We had to fashion counterforces to deal with stupid kids who wanted to fly planes into buildings—and maybe give every potential suicide bomber a JC PC, dignity, a scholarship to college, and lessons in thinking with the top head instead of the bottom one.

Although J3 had charged me with coordinating anti-terrorism, the real work fell on Ron Durondon. Durondon was no-nonsense about his approach to this stuff: "Just wipe the bastards out. Period." So, wherever we found a dictator or terrorist, Durondon assassinated him—no questions asked. Durondon hired a barber to trim more than the beard of the president of Iran; we learned that the bastard had tortured Americans during the Iranian Revolution. This sort of instant messaging motivated others not to harbor bad guys. Lip service to democracy rose—demonstrating the Machiavellian muffler effect—but I feared we were becoming more evil than counterforce required.

I worked hard to make J3 look noble while Durondon and Bull Consep did their thing. I spun the world around our own axis of justifiable evil. Still the world resisted our view of the universe. We were powerful, but even with our huge gauze- and steel-covered phallus, the rest of the world refused to appreciate our *feeling*. For one thing, not everyone made love in White House English.

White House Television tried to jump the language barrier by translating our positions to the planet. Most people with electricity had access to televisions—so if we could tune them in, we could brainwash them.

Vice President Beelzebob's JC PC giveaway had broken Olympic records and solved the ancient riddle of free products. He sold cheap subscriptions to PM—Pearless Media—an off-shoot of White House Television that transmitted news. It was like handing out free cell phones for paid air time.

Liz accidentally provided the solution for sucking in the world to our way of thinking—or rather Mr. Bobs did when Liz and I bought Robert Kennedy's estate, known as Hickory Hill, overlooking the Potomac. Mr. Bobs installed a satellite dish no larger than a hand that picked up not only TV signals, but closed Internet channels. If Robby-Bobby could build and bring billions of them to Bumfuck and make them simple to operate, J3 could massage his messianic messages.

Liz estimated that a billion restricted dishes would cost only $10 billion. But if governments got on board, they might cost nothing to the users.

So I had to convince the world governments—including our own—to support this plan. "Good idea," was all J3 said when I interrupted his group interview with his new harem. Durondon, Consep, and General Hart seemed satisfied. UN Secretary-General Bush promised to support the scheme if I called it the "Bush Dish." I test-marketed the model with a few VIPs, and somehow we came up with the cash.

We launched the free Bush Dishes with a media blitz; we sent out brains and brain waves to every country on earth. Our message was simple: "Free Satellite Television and Internet!" We declined to enlarge the small print that warned of the beaucoup bucks they would pay if they didn't want our White House claptrap.

The world snapped up the offer. To our pleasant surprise, advertisers footed not only the initial $10 billion bill but far more for a world-wide audience. We made boxcars of money that I stashed in the backyard of Hickory Hill until dollars overflowed into the sewer line and clogged the toilets. We created a market that could penetrate every television in the world. We intended to stifle information, but I also appreciated the unintended benefits of commerce.

It took less than a year to manufacture and distribute the Bush Dishes—and the economies of poor countries leaped astonishingly as a result. Businesses sprang up everywhere to install the dishes and to advertise. With the help of Russians—who cracked even the quirkiest codes—even numbskulls learned how to jerry-rig the systems to capture every Internet channel for free. Needless to say, our information limitations didn't work.

What did work was that nearly everyone on earth used the system—even animal herders with hand-cranking generators in Mongolia, the Caucasus, and the Andes. Anti-Western countries saw the benefits of advanced communication and piggy-backed their own propaganda. For the first time since the Inauguration Revolution, people praised the U.S.—and J3—for pushing useful technology. J3, Mr. Bobs, and George W. shared the Nobel Peace Prize. Again, J3 came out looking perfect—and I came out richer than Rockefeller.

In the meantime, we honed our messages—which we delivered a hundred different ways: democracy and dispute resolution were better than blowing your horny self up for sex with seventy-two honeys in heaven. The Machiavellian muffler became a metaphor for the marketplace.

Because Pearless Computer also profited by taking the lead, it grew to become the largest corporation in the history of the universe. And no one tangled with it. The more Mr. Bobs gave away, the richer he—and Liz and I—became. It was nuts—exactly the opposite of what anyone would think. But when they gave something away, they stimulated the markets—and encouraged others to buy add-ons. When people had money and security, they purchased and sold, and peace prevailed.

XXIII

The 2004 elections never appeared on the radar screen because no one bothered to run against Nobel Prize winners President James Jefferson Jones and Vice President Robert Fenster. The Democrats gave up in frustration, but that didn't stop J3 from campaigning. J3 cultivated a cult of personality with banners and bombastic endorsements everywhere he went. Fenster fabricated holograms and robots for J3 that served us faithfully in the campaign. J3 took trips to Europe and Asia, but the holograms performed better and more diplomatically back in the states. Still, J3 shined with a charisma no one could quite explain, although some said it was his George Clooney sex appeal. I just thought he put on a great show—directed by yours truly.

J3 won in a landslide that rivaled any election by a dictator: 98% of the voting electorate chose J3, with 2% voting for write-in candidates. The voter turnout hovered somewhere around 25%, which wasn't great but was still respectable in a one-party state. Al Gore received approximately 0.3% of the votes, and so did George W. Bush. John McCain beat both of them with 0.5%. I received 345 votes, Leroy 101, and Buster Keaton 2.

No doubt J3 was gaining godlike respect from the practical results of his ideology. Shortly after the election, Liz and I watched old World War II propaganda films and saw a similar adulation in the eyes of German and Soviet and Japanese women. It was strangely funny that anyone would adore an illusion more than reality. J3 hadn't changed. He still spent his spare time shacking up with young, crazed women. He was becoming, if not exactly the type of bad guy we assassinated, the peculiar sort of Ozian leader whose personal power snowballed—*Il Duce, Der Führer*, The Magnificent One. However, our Perfect President stood for democracy, peace, and freedom.

Under J3's leadership, the standard of living improved in the world. For the first time in a century, man became less destructive than nature. War and terrorism declined so sharply that populations suffered only from hurricanes, floods, earthquakes, droughts and diseases. Americans made so much money that we no longer needed programs for the poor, and Leroy quit asking for housing subsidies. Interest rates dropped enough to construct houses on every available piece of land (except the North Pole and Antarctica). The economy pulsated like King Kong's heart; capital flowed like rich, oxygenated blood; inflationary pressure remained low; market segments functioned freely and efficiently.

The global educational level rocketed with the proliferation of schools, universities, and well-paid teachers. Of course, the elderly and the sick still needed help; but with low world-wide taxes and booming economies, the burden of the infirm declined. The rising tide lifted all except a few dinghies. Life was good—all because of J3.

Granted, a few snags appeared. Natural resources suffered with prosperity. Chinese demand diminished oil supplies until non-gasoline cars proliferated. The increasing population of the world strained transportation, clean water, and infrastructure. Family organization decayed as health, wealth, and security diminished its importance.

Congress rubber-stamped all of our policies—even assassination and torture, which appeared radical during J3's first term. The world adopted J3's admiration for Machiavelli—in fact, a Vatican biology guru wrote that J3's neo-ends-justify-the-means philosophy served God because natural pain was a warning against greater harm. That endorsement allowed us to draw both the church and the evolutionists to our side of the torture issue.

International law changed to fit our policies; but the U.S., respecting other countries, joined the International Criminal Court to deal with real war criminals. We also signed the Kyoto Global Warming Treaty and worked out missile and defense protocols with Russia. Putin long since had wiped out Chechnya through torture and assassination, but hadn't quite gotten around to establishing the kind of democracy in Russia we thought essential. We considered assassinating him but couldn't find anyone more democratic to replace him.

We kept pumping out our messages, and J3 kept looking better and better. Eventually, even I came to believe in his brilliance. He not only was a visionary; he was an *invisionary* who could see things others couldn't.

In the six or seven years since I'd left Kansas Avenue, I too had become an invisionary—a serious seer of signs, a sage, a snoot. My house was the White House. I had transformed myself from powerless to powerful and had changed the world because I manipulated J3. I was also getting way too big for my Brooks Brothers britches.

Liz wanted kids, but I had Buster Keaton and no time for a baby. Besides, I would make a rotten father. How could I teach kids right from wrong when I didn't know myself? Despite my successes in power and money, I was still a narcissist who didn't care what happened to others. I made things materialize just to push limits. I read a terabyte of tomes by bloggers about my insufficiencies. I slept at night only because I ignored the suffering of others. Liz naturally became upset about all of this. "Look, Smitty, you're not as depraved as you think. You care about right and wrong. You care about me."

Of course I cared about Liz. And I did get a kick out of helping the world through J3. But I was realistic: I wasn't an upright person. Not like Liz, anyway. Not like Mother Theresa, or the do-gooders of the world. I saw life as a struggle, and I was one of the tough guys. Liz moderated me—and I knew it. But I didn't want her to keep me from my work. If I really softened my attitude, the world could fall apart.

"What do you want?" Liz finally asked. "If you had one wish, what would it be?"

"A good beer," I said. But I didn't even want that. I used to think I wanted a house when I was homeless. Then a job when I was jobless. Then Liz when I was Lizless. I wanted what I didn't have. Now that I had everything, I didn't want anything more.

"Kids," she said. "You want kids—because kids force you to express real values."

"You're reading too many of our ads," I answered. But she was almost right. If I wanted kids, it was only to repair the damage to humanity I had caused. I capitulated, and we had quintuplets—all boys—and I became a proud dad. We named them J5 (for Jason Ward Smith V), J6, J7, J8 and J9.

By 2006, give or take a few natural disasters in Louisiana and Pakistan—and a scandal in which Ron Durondon accidentally shot a fellow hunter and blamed him for getting in the way—life at the center of the universe stabilized. J3 did only what he wanted, which was have sex ten times a day. We took care of everything else. JC technology provided a hundred ways to avoid J3's actual presence. We agreed to treaties with signature machines; gave his speeches with voice and animation machines; conducted meetings with holograms, robots, computer images, and videos. Robby-Bobby perfected a mechanical double of J3 that not only walked and talked like J3, but sweated the same compounds.

J3 seemed oblivious to his talent for disappearing. He no longer read briefings and *never* called meetings. He seldom traveled and missed appointments with foreign leaders. He trusted me—and I reciprocated by making him look perfect without his presence. Every part of the administration did its own thing—and took its responsibility seriously. J3 didn't want to deal with anything more complex than choosing a sandwich or a girl, but we still issued media reports that he was working hard.

Long-suffering Linda eventually tried to warn him that his seclusion would hurt more than his causes. But J3 had grown so addicted to philandering that she couldn't gain his attention for more than a few minutes. She once wrote him a note to leave on his desk. The note said, "Jimmy Jeff, I've had it. Go fuck yourself and the girl you rode in on. Linda." However she stumbled over him on the carpet of the Oval Office with the girl he rode in on. Linda dropped the note on his naked body—careful not to dig her heels into his back. The girl *du jour's* face showed slight embarrassment, and she winked at Linda to ask for something like forgiveness. Linda simply wrote out another note and dropped it on her: "Bimbo Number 4,341!"

J3, of course, relied on Clinton's affair with Monica to give him his free ride. I lost track of his nubilettes—except those that possessed size forty-five breasts or an IQ over a hundred. J3 had become ridiculously indiscriminate. Occasionally I interviewed his aspirants before their sacrifice to the Wiz, and sometimes I hardly contained my own *feeling*. Since J3 didn't intend to see any of the girls again, his prime concern became making sure they didn't raise hell when he kicked them out. Although his selection process reminded me of a whale gobbling up plankton, he sometimes requested a brightly colored minnow or a hard-charging piranha. I chose his lunch with the shallowest of criteria—such as whether a target wore short skirts or revealed enough cleavage.

One memorable candidate was a true professional—as I discerned from the heading of her résumé: "Point of Contact Personal Relations Manager." When I asked for more specifics, she leaned over my desk to present her surgical investments. "Is that specific enough?" I passed her along to J3 with my recommendation. J3 didn't compensate her; but since she had implant loans to repay, I put her to work with the bean counters in the IRS.

In short, the White House turned into the Whore House—and Uncle Sam paid the bills.

This extra-curricular activity naturally interfered with running the country. From time to time, a senator or congressman insisted on meeting with J3 to rubber-stamp legislation. In critical times, we forced J3 to appear—but usually

I asked Mr. Bobs to stand in. Once we tried using the J3 robot, but it sweated so much it shorted out in mid-sentence and held its position for nearly an hour before a medical team hauled it away. After a few of these episodes, no one much cared about J3. To the news media, J3 conjured up images of Nero and Emperor Hirohito—closed away and too eccentric to deal with mundane things such as running a country.

The public eventually grew concerned with J3's odd behavior, but we spun our way past that, too. We staged White House Television programs and set up Web sites to spread folksy propaganda. Despite the bugs in the J3 robot, Robby-Bobby's ability to re-create every aspect of J3 became so polished that we didn't need J3 at all. In fact, J3 remained clueless about the stuff we put out under his name. We claimed that the Perfect President was very busy, writing policy or winging away on a plane. J3 did take lots of trips—but mostly with his penis.

Beelzebob didn't like it one bit, although he contributed the technology to make it all happen. However, even he possessed little power—other than his corporate power—to change things. Liz didn't go for the situation either. She wrote off J3 as a hedonist and focused instead on my influence over his policies. She ragged on me to launch legislative reforms, which I did in a mix of liberal and conservative presidential directives that I forged with J3's signature machine. I convinced Paul Rivers to provide the White House an opinion that said our unitary executive could disregard any law that conflicted with my ability to carry out—well—the laws.

XXIV

In the fall of 2006, it all began to unravel. One crisp, clear day, J3 asked me to ride with him to Camp David in his helicopter. When we arrived, we hiked the red-and-yellow hills surrounding the retreat. J3 wore jeans and boots. I wore a sharp Armani suit and Moreschi leather-soled shoes. J3 climbed up hills, and I slipped down them on my ass. After a while, J3 let on that he had a serious personal problem. I expected him to ask me to arrange a tryst with some actress, but he told me he wasn't pissing right, had passed blood, and was afraid he'd caught something. He wanted me to set up a doctor's visit—all absolutely and totally secret.

I'd known a street doctor by the name of Dr. Axel Hatchet—pronounced "Ha-Che," unlike the axe and more like the cohort of Castro—but hadn't had any contact for years. Although he'd never been afraid of much, he took ridiculous chances by selling drugs through his Che Guevara Free Clinic. He'd saved himself from arrest more than a few times because his patients protected him. Leroy and I always admired his edginess; I first met him after a serious fight. I always had paid Dr. Hatchet cash—what little I had. Leroy quit going to him for his diabetes when he obtained health insurance and Dr. Hatchet refused to process the paperwork. "Insurance is a capitalist plot," he perfunctorily explained.

So I called the legendary street doctor. "Dr. Hatchet, this is Smitty—Jason Smith."

"Never heard of you."

"Sure you have. I used to see you when I needed a prescription. I'm friends with Leroy Stivers, the Secretary of HUD."

"Who are you again?"

"I just told you. Smitty. I'm the chief of staff to the President of the United States."

"Right—and I'm the Surgeon General. Let me guess. You want me to operate on the president?"

"First I want you to examine him. Then you can operate if necessary."

Dr. Hatchet guffawed. "Sure, why not? After I cut up the Perfect President, I can do the whole UN, starting with that international idiot George W." He hung up on me.

Regardless of the rebuff, the president's chopper dropped Deuce Brucie and me at Bolling Air Force Base on the Potomac. From there we drove to Dr. Hatchet's run-down clinic in Anacostia. According to the independent checks Deuce Brucie ran on the run down from Camp David, Dr. Hatchet still held a license.

The Che Guevara Free Clinic came up short on chairs, receptionists, and patients when Deuce and I arrived—as if someone had warned them to clear out. But I heard movement in the back rooms. I shouted, and the doc emerged wearing a Ha-Che Guevara beard and beret and looking a lot older than I remembered. He said he'd removed the chairs to keep people from hanging around too long and fired the receptionist because she didn't charge anyone, drank too much, and couldn't make appointments.

Dr. Hatchet gazed through me and my mud-stained suit as though my pieces didn't fit. I told him again that I was Smitty, Leroy's friend. Then he recalled me—sort of. "Yeah—you were the smart one—or the stupid one," he said. "You chose to be homeless. You could have done so much with your life, but you elected to live in the 'hood. I always wondered what happened to you."

"I work for the President of the United States."

"I knew J3 was insane. He probably has syphilis like Napoleon."

"He's passing blood, so maybe he's got something like it." I explained why Dr. Hatchet needed to come with us. He put together a bag of medical instruments and drugs and locked the doors of the clinic. On the helicopter flight to Camp David, Dr. Hatchet sat speechless in J3's seat.

When we touched down, Deuce Brucie's Secret Service detail searched him and directed him to sign thirty-something documents. I led him to one of the cabins reserved for foreign dignitaries. Even Dr. Hatchet, who had seen everything in DC, let his jaw flap when he viewed J3 for the first time. "Holy Fidel!" he exclaimed, "I guess you weren't lying for once."

J3 thanked Dr. Hatchet for coming but kept referring to him as Dr. Guevara. "I've got some medical problems, Dr. Guevara, that I have to keep secret from everyone, including my wife. I think my dick is falling off."

Dr. Hatchet pursed his lips. "We call it the Pinocchio effect. You tell so many fibs that it keeps growing until it drops off." Dr. Hatchet examined him while I waited outside with Deuce Brucie. After an hour, Dr. Hatchet called me back in. J3 slouched glumly in a reclining chair. "We'll need tests, but it looks like President Jones either has a serious prostate problem or a textbook of sexually transmitted diseases. He said he's been banging lots of girls. He ought to use condoms. You can get them at any drugstore. I told him they were invented in Babylonia when the shepherds did more to the sheep on a cold night than count them."

"Prostate problem or STD, I've just been fucked in a whole new way," J3 complained. "I hope it's a prostate problem—even cancer. I can explain that."

"Good luck," both Dr. Hatchet and I said at the same time.

"Jesus F. Christ, Smitty, you make goddamn sure we explain this right."

"Mr. President, I don't think we should explain anything unless someone finds out first."

After mulling over the options, Dr. Hatchet told J3 he would take the blood samples back to DC and have them analyzed. J3 wanted none of that and insisted that Deuce Brucie take the blood to a local hospital in Waynesboro. "Anyone who has ever visited Waynesboro will remember the nearby Blue Ridge Mountains—and that's about all."

Off Deuce Brucie and company went in two SUVs. While we waited, I imagined Liz saying, "See, I told you his prick would wither away." Dr. Hatchet ruminated over this special visit to the *sanctum sanctorum* of presidential privacy. J3 worried about the loss of his pastime and, except for some mild Tourette's outbursts, was amiable to Dr. Hatchet. But J3 kept apologizing for knocking off Castro.

The results confirmed that J3 had enough bugs to infect half the world. According to Deuce, the Waynesboro hospital demanded (unsuccessfully) the name of the blood donor and threatened to notify the Center for Disease Control of a pandemic. Dr. Hatchet concluded that J3 needed to launch a preemptive strike of massive doses of antibiotics and anti-viral drugs. Dr. Hatchet also needed to biopsy J3's prostate and to relieve the pressure on his urethra. I suggested a female urologist, but J3 was afraid that the news would leak as fast as his bladder—so he insisted that Dr. Guevara operate.

I arranged for the hospital in Waynesboro to host the surgery. The Secret Service dumped their men-in-black suits for jeans and drove us to the hospital. Dr. Hatchet checked J3 in as Steven Albert, but the hospital staff remained leery. "Who are these guys?" one resident asked as the Secret Service marched down a corridor to the operating rooms. To say the least, Dr. Hatchet had no operating privileges, and I doubted whether he was up to the challenge of cutting the Perfect President. He hadn't seriously operated on anyone for a decade. But it was the presidential ding-a-ling, so J3 could entrust it to whomever.

The small team of doctors assembled, and J3 kidded around with them like Reagan until the anesthesia took affect. For reasons beyond anything I could ever figure out, J3 suffered some sort of colossal breakdown and died right there on the table. Needless to say, Dr. Hatchet was pretty upset—"I just killed the President of the United States"—but the rest of the doctors told Dr. Hatchet these things happened from time to time and that he shouldn't worry about it.

Meanwhile, I sat outside the operating room with the Secret Service guys. After a few hours, we began to wonder what was taking so long. When Dr. Hatchet finally emerged looking ashen and told me that J3 had passed to the other side, I thought he was joking—but then I saw J3's body. We all stared at one another. Finally, Deuce Brucie asked what we should do.

"Don't do anything for two minutes," I said, "until I catch my breath."

I tried to think, but thinking was difficult. What would the country—not to mention the world—do if it found out that the most powerful leader in the world had croaked because of a botched prostate operation necessitated by syphilis and gonorrhea? It would revolt. "Look," I finally said, "move the body to the morgue here. As far as the world knows, J3 is still at Camp David."

The hospital insisted on doing an autopsy on Steven Albert, and it turned out he was a lot sicker than anyone suspected. His brain showed lesions that explained some of his recent craziness. He had a bad heart and was allergic to the anesthesia. He had HIV, syphilis, gonorrhea and herpes. So there was plenty of contributory self-indulgence to exculpate even the most negligent doctor, including the White House quacks who phonied-up J3's physical every year. Fortunately, I felt no guilt because I was still a sociopath and, well, this was just one more death. This was a big death, no question about it, but still just a run-of-the-mill ordinary I-didn't-take-care-of-myself presidential death.

The Secret Service moved J3, as Steven Albert, to the morgue while Dr. Hatchet, Deuce Brucie, and I returned to Washington on the presidential helicopter. Deuce agreed that everyone had to shut up; any statement whatsoever could endanger the security of the United States. He threatened Dr. Hatchet with a horrible death if he said anything. Dr. Hatchet was pretty cool. He'd been threatened so often it hardly fazed him. Even the technically new president, my brother-in-law Robert "Beelzebob" Fenster, couldn't know his new status. That meant I couldn't let in Liz, who instantly would blab.

But somehow I thought the right thing to do was tell her. I invited Liz to the White House. When she showed up, I couldn't generate the courage to say anything. As much as I loved her, I knew she would convince her brother to dump all of J3's hard-fought policies. I stalled and then asked her, finally, if she wanted to go to dinner. She looked puzzled by my patter, but I fixed that by closing my office door and making love to her on my desk. "That's a hell of way to ask me to dinner," she said after we flattened the foreign policy of Burkina Faso. "You sure know how to show a girl a good time."

At one of the best restaurants in Washington, I stared at my plate and said almost nothing except, "How are J5 through J9?" What could I do? What *would* I do? Everyone thought J3 was still at Camp David. Even if I couldn't tell Liz, I had to let Linda Jones in on the secret. She would know something was wrong with her husband.

I sent Liz home, went back to my White House office, and called Linda, who slept soundly in the residence. She met me in a sexy silk robe and led me to a sitting room. "What's so important?"

"I've got some bad news—J3's dead."

Linda stared at me. "What do you mean he's dead?"

"He's dead. He had a prostate operation and died."

"You're kidding, aren't you?" Linda peered past me as if someone else were talking. "You came up here to sleep with me."

"Linda, the president is dead."

It took twenty minutes before she heard me, and even then she didn't believe me.

"Why wasn't this on the news? Why didn't someone tell me earlier?"

"Because we need to keep this a secret. It affects the security of the entire world. The world will come apart if it learns that J3's dead."

"Where is he?"

"In Waynesboro, Pennsylvania."

"Take me up there. I want to see him."

I arranged for the president's helicopter to pick us up on the lawn of the White House and fly us back to Camp David. From there we climbed into a tinted SUV, and Deuce Brucie drove us to Waynesboro. We arrived in the middle of the night, but Deuce managed to get us into the hospital morgue. Visiting a morgue anytime—especially in the middle of the night—was something I didn't like. The attendant didn't recognize Linda as the first lady or realize that Steven Albert was J3. When he rolled out the naked body, J3 had a big grin on his face, not unlike the one plastered on Dominique-Pierre Surlepont, and scars all over his chest and crotch. Linda kept calling the body "my president," and soon even the attendant began to figure things out. Still, it was too bizarre for the President of the United States to be lying on a Waynesboro slab.

We returned to Camp David and met with Ron Durondon, Bull Consep, General Hart, and Paul and Sarah Rivers, who had arrived in a string of helicopters. As dawn broke, we decided that only J3 and his administration could hold the world together. Everyone liked Mr. Bobs, but we agreed that he would let the political dynamic go to hell. Paul, the attorney general, resisted hiding J3's death. "Under the law, Fenster already is the president. Denying him the office is tantamount to a coup."

Paul had a point. But Robby-Bobby wasn't the president if J3 hadn't died. Steve Albert had died, but not James Jefferson Jones. Since J3's term was up in only two more years anyway, it made perfect sense to keep the Perfect President alive until then. "We have a robot and holograms—we don't need *him*."

"Someone will leak the news," General Hart feared. "Too many people already know."

"We'll just have to be careful," Durondon replied.

Linda was pretty upset, of course, but not as disturbed as I would have imagined. She realized she could continue living in the White House with full benefits as the first lady. Maybe more if Harriet Horsehead could find some new men. Sarah was sad at first, but then she appreciated that details of her affair with J3 had died with him. I hoped J3 hadn't willed her any of his bugs, that I hadn't caught any from Sarah, and that Liz hadn't caught any from me.

For the next few days, we conspired to keep J3's death from the world and to prevent J3's improprieties from provoking a world-wide panic.

XXV

Linda and I arranged for the burial of Steve Albert in a simple grave in a Waynesboro cemetery. No one except the Secret Service agents had any idea the body laid in the ground was the President of the United States. The undertaker said he noticed a resemblance to the president, but in the same breath passed it off as a coincidence—even when Linda (who looked exactly like the first lady) referred to Albert as Jimmy Jeff.

After the burial, I selected those who needed to know about J3 and those who didn't. Fortunately, Deuce Brucie and his Secret Service agents kept the secret, which explained the reason for their title. J3's personal secretary needed to know—after all, she had to write letters to his girlfriends asking them not to come around any longer and, oh, by the way, get checked for every STD known to humankind.

We created an inner circle—and an outer one. The inner one consisted of those who could "keep the secret." Those we doubted left for Guantanamo to "keep the secret." It was a drastic step, but world peace rested on my decisions. By the time I finished the selection, only a hundred or so actually knew—but that was still too many. And a leak could occur anywhere. I understood now why Nixon had created the Plumbers.

I didn't tell Mr. Bobs or Liz anything. In order to safeguard the secret, I sent the vice president on useless errands and limited Liz's access to the White House. I recognized that this sort of restriction would wreck me eventually, because Liz had more intuition than a tarot card reader and probably would find out on her own. Nevertheless, I couldn't afford the risk now of her telling her brother. Another coup could easily occur, and we needed a smooth transfer to Beelzebob when the time was right. We needed two years.

The new relationship with the first lady started off as rocky as Niagara Falls because she drained money as quickly and determinedly as the falls drained the Niagara River—even faster now that J3 abruptly had stopped complaining. I signed her weekly checks with J3's automatic pen, but Linda demanded all of his cash as well. She threatened to blow the whole thing if I resisted—and I considered packing *her* off to the beaches of Guantanamo. She obviously wasn't above blackmail, but she knew I could blackmail her, too—or worse if I could overcome my stunted conscience. Even so, within a few months I signed over most of J3's funds. J3 had been paying his girlfriends hush money—so following suit with Linda didn't affront my microscopic morality. Besides, if someone was entitled to hush money, Linda ought to stand first in line.

Blackmail became a regular part of the White House; but considering the price of world peace, it wasn't much.

I had greater problems with personal appearances, constituent support, and congressional endorsements. The dead president declined everything that required his appearance, but we now had to dance faster than ever to contain the pressure. We sent letters, souvenirs, and kitschy stuff to neutralize the natives. We let those who kept the secret use our technology to record J3's voice in order to push their positions or to provide proof to the press that the Perfect President wanted some product. I suspected that Robby-Bobby and Pearless Computers were working on even more advanced replications, but Liz told me nothing.

We got by—and improved the voice synthesizer to emulate every J3 nuance. When I spoke into a microphone hooked to a JC computer, my voice came out exactly as J3's, inflections and all. Although everyone in the White House learned about our hoax, Congress never quite caught on, and neither did those who couldn't keep some part of the secret. I was becoming the Wizard of Oz.

Of course, I couldn't do everything alone and had to share the Wizard's title. I appropriated the moniker "General Wizard"—but smart-alecks referred to me as J4, and it stuck. Durondon adopted the title "Foreign Policy Wizard." Sarah came back to the White House to become the "Domestic Wizardess." She proved the most adept at responding to off-the-cuff questions intended for J3. She built a control room for the system, just like the Wizard in the movie, and hooked the synthesizer to one of the J3 robots. When the robot opened its mouth—usually like Frankenstein—out came Sarah's thoughts in J3's sharp, witty, and perfectly-inflected voice.

Leroy was the first outer-circle person to confront me with his certainty that J3 had kicked the bucket: "Smitty, we both know that J3 has long since departed."

"How do you know?" I asked.

"Because the White House doesn't bullshit me any longer. The J3 Administration is keeping its promises—so power must have passed to the J4 Administration."

I brought him into the inner circle, gave him the secret handshake, and confessed to being one of the Wizards of Oz.

"As long as you aren't a wizard of the KKK, I'm OK with it. Maybe you can get your conscience now that you hand out virtues. When folks learn that J3 is gone, they'll throw the biggest party the world has ever seen."

"The world loves J3. Besides, no one will find out."

"No one except Russia, China, Europe, Africa, and South America, including some ruby-shoed chick who wrecks everything. We may have to walk back to Kansas Avenue some day."

We didn't walk back then, despite the seepage from the leaky inner circle. I managed a magnificent government and tried every trick to fool the American people. White House Television issued daily reports filled with bogus videos, holograms, actors, and robots, all showing J3 as the most active president of the twenty-first century—traveling, meeting with his cabinet, kissing babies, negotiating treaties, taking a romantic vacation with Linda. J3 led the country through natural disasters and a war or two. As General Wizard, I shaped his life as the Perfect President. I was J3—and J4 too. I was the Perfect President.

Sure—skeptics appeared and questioned J3's policies. To the extent they didn't push too hard, I put up with them. But if they asked too many embarrassing questions, I sent them on tax-payer-paid vacations to Bumfuck. The non-spin media asked for news conferences, and we perfected electronic ones—"e-conferences"—where J3 sat in the Oval Office and batted softballs thrown from the press room.

Because of my demanding schedule as chief of staff and General Wizard, I spent little time with Liz and less with my young sons, J5 through J9. I brought aging Buster Keaton into the White House to keep me company. Liz grew seriously upset, especially after Sarah returned to the White House. Liz pressed me to explain J3's absences—because, she said, she and her brother suspected more than I was telling them. I kept answering that he was becoming a recluse. Liz told me that I was turning into a recluse myself with her and the kids, that I had become far more distant than she had ever been. In a fit of anger, Liz took off with the kids to Chicago to live in the Fenster mansion. I tried to reconcile with her, but she wanted no part of a J3 Washington any longer—and I couldn't leave.

Robby-Bobby's loyalty toward me also waned after Liz took off. He refused to fill in for J3 when I asked. "Smitty, you're becoming a little dictator. You weren't elected president."

"You're just mad at me because of Liz."

Mr. Bobs finally agreed to cover for J3, but I had to enter into a pact not to curtail his political activities—which included, as I discovered from Deuce Brucie, his pursuit of the Republican nomination for president in 2008. I left him alone, but he told the world that J3 needed to curb the power of his staff. That kicked off a firestorm of tricky questions aimed not only at the elusive J3, but at me and the entire inner circle. I had to prove that J3 was healthy and still in charge. I ordered White House Television to produce a phony video of J3 visiting Potemkin Children's Hospital in southern Russia with General Hart, Ron Durondon, and Linda.

Sooner or later, despite our valiant efforts, the American people grew impossibly restive and demanded a credible explanation from J3 for the weird lapses in leadership. I wasn't sure what to do—although Durondon just said, "fuck 'em all."

Vladimir Putin, who had become "President for Life of Greater Russia," provided an unintended opportunity when he expressed his irritation with J3 for sneaking into the Potemkin Villages. He demanded an invitation to the White House to protest. When I told him that J3 couldn't meet with him because he was sick, Putin was insulted, and he delivered his complaints to the world press. The media believed J3 was in perfect health—after all, J3 had just visited Russia. Of course, J3 had no health problems: he was dead. In response, however, White House Television produced an entire video novel, complete with plots and heroes, highlighting J3's battles with his overactive glands. We called it *My Struggle*. I told Putin that despite the unintended slights, J3 was indeed ailing.

Finally, after a few sleepless nights discussing strategy with Buster Keaton, I let Putin meet with J3; but he would have to keep the secret of J3's most recent relapse. I knew, as Russians instinctively knew, that illness diminishes the decisiveness of a dictator. But I decided to "Leninize" J3. I would stuff him in a glass box—or better yet, a plastic bubble—and animate him.

I considered digging him up from the Waynesboro cemetery, waxing him to a fine lifelike polish, and parking him next to a speaker; but then I realized it would take more to revitalize the real him than gussying up some good J3 machine. We needed our best J3 robot, a lot of make-up, and the collective Wizards' skills to answer tough questions.

Because Robby-Bobby had moved away from us—and blocked our unlimited use of Pearless technology—we brought in the Small World Amusement Park folks to synchronize the robot's expressions with remote controls. The Small World engineers used a different technology that didn't work right; J3's mouth contorted like a bad actor in an old Japanese horror film. If I voiced something through the synthesizer, like, "Good to see you," J3's lips twitched about two seconds late, the eyes fluttered as if he were flirting, and out popped, "God damn you!" Fortunately, smart people could fix anything, and before long Sarah convinced even me that J3 was still alive: she made him groan.

Sarah dressed the robot in pajamas and a robe and propped him up in a chair behind a glass wall in the residence. A bottle of water rested on a table with pill containers and the current *Washington Post*—as if J3 spent his free time hanging around his plastic bubble drinking water, popping pills, and reading the news. We set up another chair outside the bubble for Putin and adjusted the many cameras, including the ones in J3's eyes, to watch the fun. Sarah, Durondon, and I crowded into the Wizard control room with its dials and levers.

Secretary of State General Hart greeted the Russian president when his helicopter landed on the White House lawn and told Putin that J3 was ready to see him from his plastic-enclosed quarantine bubble—necessitated by a major viral infection.

"Will he recover?" Putin asked.

"Of course," replied General Hart. "He's a great athlete."

"Like Mao Tse-Tung," added Putin.

"More like R2D2."

Military, Secret Service and Russian security personnel escorted Putin and his translator to the Perfect President and hacked their way through the wires, tubes, air ducts and other nonsense we rigged to con Putin. I took the controls of the robot, stood him up from his chair in a show of respect, and then sat him down. Putin cleared out the wires, took a drink of water, and toasted J3 with another. I fumbled with J3's hands trying to open the bottle of water and then spilled everything on the floor, apologizing with an "Oh, shit!" for being a klutz. If J3 had taken a drink, he would have shorted out—and instead of toasting Putin, he would have toasted himself.

"Mr. President," Putin mumbled through his translator, "I'm sorry to see you in such an ill state. Are you all right?"

"Thanks for asking, Vlad," I said through J3. "I'm OK—just a very violent infection."

"What sort of infection? We have great doctors that might assist yours."

"I know you have great doctors, but even they can't help in a matter as serious as this. As you can see, viruses affect world relationships."

"What virus is it? Do you know? And how could you have contracted it?" Putin smiled. "I've heard that your friends may have given you some unwanted gifts." Putin winked at J3.

J3 just sat there looking stupid—which meant backstage in the Wizard control room I was feeling pretty stupid. Should I move his arms and legs into an uncomfortable position? Should I make him wink back? Hell, I didn't know the controls for winking or even if we had them. I just stared at the blinking lights and levers, wondering which buttons to push. Finally I pushed a random button—probably the panic button—and J3's elbow flew up in a "Heil Hitler!" salute.

A look of horror spread over Putin's face. "The virus is doing very strange things."

"Why do you keep talking about the virus?" I had J3 inquire as politely as I could.

"Because we want to make sure you're healthy and the virus doesn't spread. If it can infect the President of the United States, it can infect the presidents of other countries."

"It won't spread," J3 said.

"Again, what is it?"

I grimaced at Sarah and she shrugged.

"Ebola," J3 replied. "A virus that destroys the muscle and tissue in a body. Fortunately, it hasn't done that to me because, as you can see, my body is made of abnormally strong material." I then knocked the robot's hands against its chest and got a metallic and plastic sound.

"Ebola? How is it possible?"

Not only was Putin incredulous, but both Sarah and Durondon reacted as if I had lost my mind. Durondon tried to grab the microphone for the J3 voice, but I pulled it away. Sarah just sat down and started laughing. I was afraid the sound would carry over to the robot. I regained my composure.

"I don't know," J3 said, "but you can see our dilemma."

"And you will be OK? We're not going to have a situation where we need to talk to a different president anytime soon?"

"Of course not. We have a cure, but it just takes time. It has strange side effects—such as temporary loss of muscle control. But look how well I'm doing."

"Except for the jerky muscle movements, it appears you're doing well. You're more lucid than normal, in fact."

"Thank you," I replied as I accidentally hit another lever and J3 crossed and uncrossed his legs three times, as if he had to pee. "I have to rely on my staff for many things now. I hope you understand." I was now improvising so fast that I didn't have any idea what I would say next. Nether did Sarah or Durondon, who couldn't take any more. Durondon shoved me aside and took over.

"Mr. Putin," he began as J3, "let's talk about arms control. We think Russia should disarm completely and let the U.S. police the world."

"What?" Putin was aghast.

"You heard me."

"You call me Vlad one minute and then Mr. Putin when we get down to business?"

"OK, Vlad—whatever you want—we want to police the planet. You should disarm."

"Where does this request come from? We were talking about Ebola, and out of the blue you're talking about the United States ruling the world. I think you may have other problems because of the Ebola. No offense, Mr. President."

"No offense taken. But we need to get down to the important issues. Time is short."

"What does that mean?" Putin asked. "Is this Ebola more serious than you're telling me?"

"Forget about the fucking Ebola! We need to talk about nuclear proliferation—India and Pakistan nearly blew themselves up in 2001—and all those nut cases in Africa and the Middle East."

Putin looked at some notes and then said, "Why don't we talk about trade? It's less consequential to world security. Let's skip military issues for the moment."

Durondon handed the controls to Sarah—and I watched a master. She worked the controls like a symphony conductor and knew Jimmy Jeff well enough to conjure up authentic J3 gestures. She had him stand, made him fart (for which he excused himself), and then he scratched his crotch. Putin and the translator looked on in amazement.

"Mr. Jones, I think this illness is getting to you. Perhaps we should meet later. I would like to meet with Vice President Fenster, if you think that is appropriate."

"Vlad—normally I wouldn't tell you to do that, but under the circumstances, this might be a good idea."

Putin stood up unceremoniously and left shaking his head. I stared at Sarah and Durondon. "Well, I guess we're in for it now."

XXVI

The headlines of the *Washington Post* blared, "J3 QUARANTINED FOR EBOLA!" Below that: "President Claims U.S. Has Cure—But Won't Reveal It."

This was bad news because now we had to lie our way out of more trouble or discover an anti-Ebola cure, whichever came first. But Ebola was also good news because it explained J3's absences and kept the nosy world at bay. Still, the public wanted to know the condition of their Perfect President. How could he possibly have contracted the disease? Who was treating him? What did this mean to the country?

As usual, we resolved most of the problems by manipulating the news. White House Television put out special reports on the disease, possible cures, J3's work while quarantined in his bubble. We spit out so many reports that the regular media wearied of our fabrications and eventually buried them next to the foreclosures or on some Web page selling plants. We didn't convey the "Big Lie" as much as the alternative universe—the deconstruction of reality.

Big or little, the lies bogged us down. One inconsistent fact opened the door to another and left me tracking fantasies I couldn't refabricate. Unpredictable twists added to the confusion—such as the dunderheaded doctor in Dubuque who declared he donated J3's blood to a blood bank. This nonsense led to the destruction of blood supplies all across the U.S. and endangered thousands of people. I spent time I didn't have convincing Congress to appropriate emergency funds for the unnecessary screening of J3's blood.

Events overwhelmed us at the White House. I enlisted more EMTs to write public lies while I handled the mounting private ones J3 left in his will. It turned out that J3 ran so many scams attaching his nuts and bolts—and received so many kickbacks—he lost track of his debtors and creditors. They sued him. J3's lawyers needed access to him, so I had to decipher his personal accounts and write more bogus letters. I couldn't understand J3's business dealings at all, but he definitely wasn't a perfect businessman. My accounting mistakes probably cost Linda millions; but as a street person from Kansas Avenue, I did my best.

And then, like a poorly spun ball of yarn, all the lies unraveled. J3's former girlfriends brought a class action suit for the anticipated agony from Ebola. And then their significant others requested judicial injunctions against the disease and demanded damages for the loss of sexual relations. They accused J3 of becoming a one-man epidemic. J3's poll numbers dropped so low that Jimmy Carter and Hillary Clinton seemed popular with Republicans.

My brother-in-law, Robby "Mr. Bobs" Fenster, the rightful president, became positively gleeful and assumed the reins of government I dropped. This was OK with me because my hands were busy writing bogus checks and bullshit.

Before long, the country evolved from disgust to outright panic. Americans stopped having sex, and the birthrate fell to zero. The drop rattled a business community and government that depended on future consumers and taxpayers. The stock market crashed. Despite the *Sturm und Drang*, not one real case of Ebola emerged. The smartest doctors in the U.S. scratched their heads because, for the first time in history, a pandemic occurred without a disease. But that didn't stop the worst biological terror of history.

Spiteful sexual speculation soon spooked us, and several spectators swore they saw Sarah and J3 out together. Attorney General Rivers became involved by denying a J3-Sarah liaison but then publicly castigated his wife for taking the J3 robot for a walk. Some investigative reporter drew me into the sexual scandals because—of all things—he discovered that Sarah had let me stay with her in Ocean City and in Georgetown. The free media asked whether J3 was running a White House more sexually corrupt than Kennedy's.

I issued statements, but I had as much credibility as Clinton disavowing the sex he had with "that woman." The more I denied J3's decadent deportment, the more people probed. Women testified to all kinds of ridiculous but true stories.

Some stuff wasn't completely true. A photographer produced a picture of J3 leaving an apartment at 3 AM. Unless the philandering and faithless J3 robot had a hydraulic phallus, the photo was a fake. J3 was dead, but that had no influence over the disaster. The *Washington Times,* trying to crush the *Washington Post,* exposed J3's infidelity to Linda, lambasted him for contracting Ebola from an African housekeeper who never paid Social Security taxes, and wrote him off as "Inept Jimmy Jeff."

A congressional committee finally asked for an explanation. In a report recalling the Clinton period, Congress decided it was time to impeach J3.

This was too much for the first lady, and she left town to become a rodeo announcer in Wyoming for Harriet Horsehead—who earlier had returned to roping calves when some Jacobin accused her of sleeping with J3. I assumed Linda was just angry, but she feared that the whole truth and nothing but the truth would result in a jail cell with me and half the J3 Administration.

We hired more attorneys to defend J3 before the investigative committee, but the mood in Congress turned ugly. No amount of lawyering would save him. It was one thing for a president to cheat on his wife. It was another to spend taxpayers' money spreading Ebola.

The House of Representatives impeached J3 without a dissenting vote—and then sent the matter over to the Senate for trial. Our support withered before we had a chance to test it. Even Mr. Bobs, the president of the Senate, remained strangely quiet. Liz, who still wasn't one who kept the secret, returned from Chicago with the kids to persuade me to force J3's resignation for the good of the country. I gratefully made love with my beautiful wife, but I told her I couldn't abandon J3—too much was at stake.

Finally, the trial in the Senate reached its zenith. Both sides called witnesses—some good, but mostly bad. The really bad ones participated with J3 in orgies. Based on the weight of the evidence, J3 had sex with enough women to populate New York and California.

The Senate subpoenaed both J3 and me. Using the auto-signature machine, J3 responded that his subpoena was an insult. The letters back and forth might have lined a trash can, but they did nothing to influence the Senate one way or another. I adamantly refused to let a dead J3 testify. I issued a press release, however, that said J3 wanted to get to the bottom of the matter, although he was already at the bottom of the matter.

The senators—our own Republicans—turned on us. When I arrived at Congress to testify, the Chief Justice of the United States, the former Aruban justice of the peace I had selected for ripping up a traffic ticket and naturalized on behalf of J3, swore me in with a scowl. I had to think fast; the Senators clearly wanted to shoot me. Beelzebob sat above the fray, but he learned soon enough that his own position might shift. The Senate prosecutor, Senator Rain from Maine, showed how insane everything became. He began by asking if I knew for sure that J3 had Ebola.

"He had it, but he's cured," I asserted.

"What? Who's treating him? We couldn't find anyone treating him."

"He doesn't need a doctor," I said. "His body resisted it on its own." I made a mental note to talk to Dr. Hatchet in case I needed expert medical advice to back me up.

"Has President Jones been seeing anyone on the side?" Senator Rain asked. "Or should I ask, has President Jones been infecting anyone on the side?"

The Senate erupted in laughter.

"I doubt it."

"You're protecting your boss, but we know he's been seeing women—very good looking women, young women. I present to you these photos taken on Thanksgiving, 2006. Do you see him with three different women?"

I examined them. "The likeness of President Jones is pretty good—but they're fakes."

"Why do you say that?"

"Because he wasn't anywhere on Thanksgiving—hence you can't take pictures of someone not there."

"He wasn't anywhere? Anywhere is a pretty large space. Anywhere could include the solar system or the universe."

"Then he's in heaven—or hell—because President Jones is dead as a door-nail. He died a year ago."

The entire Senate went silent. Mr. Bobs twitched because, if true, he was not only the vice president and the president of the Senate, but also the President of the United States.

"What?!" Senator Main finally shouted. "Who's running the White House?"

"I am—along with our superb staff. No wars, no conflict, great economy, great care for the poor. What more do you want?"

"A democracy, Mr. Smith. A democracy."

"Did we ever have one? Or do we have a 'spinocracy'—a government by fools for fools?"

The answer irritated Senator Rain. "Well, if anyone is a fool, it's you. When did President Jones die? And why didn't you tell the American people?"

"He died last year in an operation. We had to keep it a secret."

"Mr. Smith, you can't make up this kind of stuff. I myself saw President Jones many times."

"Smoke and mirrors."

Senator Rain splattered the floor of the House of Representatives with his glares. "Frankly, Mr. Smith, you're a liar. We should hold you in contempt. In fact, where do you get the nerve to perjure yourself so blatantly under oath? President Jones is alive."

"He's dead," I repeated. "He's as dead as the holograms that run the country."

The senators rolled their eyes in such perfect unison that the TV cameras could have recorded a Broadway show. Senator Rain continued, however: "Mr. Smith, we know the White House makes up stuff all the time, but we've ignored it because the president was once good for the country. I'm afraid you, Mr. Smith, the chief of staff, and your boss, James Jefferson Jones, have become the biggest phonies ever to occupy the White House."

"Go to hell," I stated. "We're all phonies."

"We're the Congress. We represent the people of the United States."

"That may be the problem."

Senator Geist moved the sergeant at arms to arrest me for contempt of Congress—and every senator in the chamber (except for Senator Little sleeping in the back) voted in favor. The chief justice slammed his gavel, and that abruptly concluded my testimony.

The Capitol police escorted me to the DC jail where I shared a cell with Carlos Rodriguez—who said he preferred jail to his job as a swimming instructor at the April Showers Hotel. "The women don't want to swim—they just want sex in the pool. It's too much for me." That evening, all the Internet sites, cell phones, Bush Dishes, newspapers and tom-toms in the world accused me of lying to save J3's dead ass. The irony, of course, was that I was telling the truth for the first time in years.

The scandal grew worse, and civilization demanded an appearance before Congress by J3. Sarah issued a J3 statement supporting my testimony—that he was dead and was responding as a robot. This had the effect of encouraging talk-show philosophers and lawyers to debate whether a dead person can vouch for his own death.

The Senate neared its vote on conviction. It didn't look good for J3 or me. Liz visited me in jail—and I asked her to strike a deal with Senator Pai-Laste, who controlled the Republicans.

"What sort of deal?" Liz asked. "Right now you look like a lunatic."

"Tell Senator Pai-Laste that J3 will resign if the Senate lets me out."

"Did J3 tell you that he would resign? No one can find him."

"Yes. He told me. He said, 'Smitty, I've had it with this bullshit. I'm done.'"

Liz took the news better than I expected because, regardless of what happened to me, her brother—sitting stone-faced as president of the Senate—already saw himself as the next President of the U.S. Liz threw on one of her sexiest low-cut outfits and visited Senator Pai-Laste. The Senator had been an unadulterated adulterer like J3 before joining the Senate—and despite his hot-air attacks against me and J3, he saw potential in Liz.

After a few calls to round up votes, Pai-Laste accepted my offer. J3 had to resign within twenty-four hours. The deal would keep the Republicans in power and avoid the embarrassment of a Republican conviction.

Obviously, it was hard for a president to resign when he was already dead, but J3 did something bizarre, even by my standards: he refused to resign. And I had nothing to do with it.

Just before my release from jail, the non-spin media broadcast a special announcement from the President of the United States. I was surprised that word had traveled so fast and that Sarah was stripping J3 of the presidency without my involvement. But as I watched from the day room of the DC jail, there sat J3, big as life, at his desk in the Oval Office.

"My fellow Americans, I want to clear up some misconceptions about my health and activities. As you know, our administration has faced difficult challenges and amazing successes. This administration always has been forthright in promoting freedom, democracy, and integrity. Many of you have wondered whether I have a disease, whether I am incapacitated, or whether I'm having affairs with beautiful, luscious, full-breasted women. Let me tell you that all of these assertions are untrue—that I am not ill, not incapacitated, and definitely not having affairs with anyone. I love my wife, Linda, who is right here."

The camera panned to Linda, who stood next to him smiling.

"Let me explain my absence. I have just concluded a secret but highly successful endeavor in which I have secured from every country on earth except France an Agreement for Perpetual Peace and Harmony. In order to do this, I asked President Putin to provide cover for my travels by announcing publicly that I was suffering from an illness. The media mistranslated the Russian word for illness—'bolen'—to 'Ebola,' which is completely different.

"Normally I would have corrected this right away, but I wasn't here. Vice President Fenster was taking care of business while I was conducting policy, and I felt that further explanation would have compromised my secret mission.

"With regard to being seen with women other than my wife, I have with me Kim Jong Il II, the son of the former president of North Korea, to verify that on the day of the so-called photographs, I was cooking *kimchi* with Kim and Linda in Pyongyang while concluding the conditions for Perpetual Peace and Harmony."

The cameras rotated to Kim Jong Il II and Linda, and they nodded in agreement.

"My skilled chief of staff, Jason Smith, is sitting in the slammer because of his valiant efforts to shield me and to promote planetary peace. Because of his bravery, he has admirably absorbed the anger of an angst-ridden Senate. Indeed, I can't tell you how difficult it is to watch my most loyal staffer grilled by well-meaning, but misguided people. Smitty used a literary license that I was dead. This was true in a manner of speaking. It was a metaphor that Smitty, with his advanced English degrees from Harvard and Oxford, understood. The impeachment process has been an attack on the administration and a would-be death—a death to the administration, to the country, and to world peace.

"I'm certainly not dead, as you can see and as the presence of my sexy wife and Mr. Kim Jong Il II will evidence.

"But now I would like the Senate to dismiss the charges against me and allow me to finish my last year in office before, I hope, the nation elects Vice President Fenster to continue the great work of my administration.

"We Americans must have stability in the world. Disrupting the Jones Administration serves no useful purpose. We are the most powerful nation on earth because of our openness, honesty, integrity, democratic and free values. We can't let a media that looks for flaws compromise those values. I have tried to make my administration perfect, but no one is perfect. I am not the Perfect President, as some have called me.

"So again, my fellow Americans, I ask you to call or email your senators to prohibit these preposterous proceedings. Good night and God bless you."

XXVII

Now I was stunned—and I wondered whether I would rot in jail because the White House had reneged on the deal. But who in the White House? Sarah? Ron Durondon? Unlikely. It had to be someone who kept the secret—but who? I had no idea.

Senator Pai-Laste let me out of jail anyway. I promised Carlos that I would find him better work when I returned to my office. I took a cab to the White House, but the familiar guard, my good buddy to whom I sent Christmas presents and for whose stupid kid I later wrote a recommendation to the Indiana Institute of Ingratitude, wouldn't let me in. "We're sorry, Mr. Smith, but you're restricted."

"Who says? I'm the chief of staff."

"The President of the United States."

"The president is dead," I stated.

"Well, maybe, but those are my orders. And they're signed by Jimmy Jeff Jones."

"An automatic pen wrote that signature."

I called Deuce Brucie from my cell phone, but he refused to answer. I called Sarah but couldn't reach her either—and finally I called Liz to tell her I'd been released from jail. She asked where I was.

"At the White House gate, trying to get in. They won't let me in."

"Get a taxi and come home."

On the ride to Hickory Hill, I was fuming. What was going on? Who had made that sick tape of J3 and Linda and Kim Jong Il II? Obviously, Linda and the son of the dictator that J3 assassinated knew about this—because no one could have constructed robots of them that fast.

When I arrived at Hickory Hill, Buster Keaton, old and ill now, greeted me with a wagging tail. I played with him for only a minute. My young kids, J5 through J9, seemed like strangers as they stared at me. In a chorus they began to cry while I tried vainly to calm them. Liz followed me around the house and finally ordered me to sit down. "You're out," she announced. "Robby has taken over."

"What do you mean, I'm out and Robby has taken over? Taken over from whom?"

"From you. He's the rightful President of the United States and he's going to restore the country to sanity."

"He can't do that yet. Sanity will mess up everything!"

"Smitty—he and I knew all about J3's death last year. I knew *you* couldn't tell me—the Secret Service serves the president, not the chief of staff. Everyone needed J3 alive—even Robby—until we could finish the Agreement for Perpetual Peace and Harmony. You thought you were keeping my brother from becoming president while you rode out the term, but Robby was more concerned with the welfare of the United States and the world. He kept his own secrets from your cabal. Robby was afraid his work would go down the tubes if America learned the jaded truth about J3. Robby will become the next president—he technically is the President of the United States—and he really will be perfect. He identifies with the spirit of the country. He magnanimously attributed his tireless efforts to J3. He needed J3 to finish the term. But J3 is so damaged, he and his dead body need to move out of the way."

"Mr. Bobs produced the media piece?"

"Not bad, was it? He used your techniques."

"What about the impeachment proceedings? He's not going to let the Senate end J3's term, is he?"

"He's got that covered. As president of the Senate he'll dismiss the charges, and the Senate will exonerate J3. We'll wait a week or so, and then J3 will die trying to do a good deed. He'll lie in state, be buried at Arlington—and the country will mourn him as a hero. Robby will take the oath of office as president and run the country in the way the founders expected. We'll have peace and freedom and democracy and a great business climate."

Liz became more excited as she spoke, and her chest heaved. In fact, the more excited she became, the more excited I became. Despite all the anxiety and anger, my *feeling* impelled me to jump on her right there and then—but I didn't. Who said that power wasn't an aphrodisiac?

"The hell with J3. What about me?" I asked. "Will I have a job? What about us?"

"We'll be fine—except we won't stay together any longer. You have plenty of money. You can live your life with Buster Keaton, and I'll enjoy mine as the White House advisor to the president."

I stared at Liz. She had been a perfect wife—honest, decent, loyal, moral, forthright. "What has happened?" I finally asked. I didn't believe I was listening to this—all the years, all the I-love-yous, the kids. All gone just because I was a lying, no-good sociopath and her brother was launching a counter-coup?

Liz calmed down, but she retained that special *Mädchen* aura that I loved so much. "Nothing has happened. Robby has a destiny to help the world. Now, I would like you to leave."

"What about my clothes? What about J5 through J9?"

"They'll be fine."

"They're my kids, too. They have my name."

"I've changed their names. From now on, they'll be honest and transparent Fensters with no J numbers: Lincoln, Lucien, Laertiades, LeMonde and Lyman. You'll visit them when it's appropriate."

From the back of the house, Secret Service agents appeared—including Deuce Brucie—and escorted me to my car. Deuce Brucie told me to get out of Dodge. I saw the betrayal. "And you too, Deuce Brucie?" I asked.

"It's your own damn fault for sending J3 to that quack doctor. You know I couldn't support a coup. Fenster became president the minute that whacko killed J3."

I drove away as instructed, found a bed and breakfast near Baltimore, and moved in. Miranda de Veranda ran the place—and she warned me not to tear up my room or the cute doilies on the furniture. The Senate dismissed all charges against J3—with a profound apology. The Senate then passed a grandiose resolution hailing J3's achievements.

But I wasn't done. If Beelzebob could commandeer J3, so could I. I bided my time until Halloween and then called Leroy at HUD and asked him to meet me after dark with a pickup truck and a couple of shovels. "What's up?" he asked when he arrived at our meeting place. "Not finished with the J3 Revolution? I saw that Mr. Bobs is making improvements to the J3 robot. J3 must wonder who's going to push his buttons next."

"He won't wonder long," I said. "Let's go trick or treating." Leroy drove me to a Wal-Mart where I bought masks, markers, and signboards. We then headed up to J3's grave in Waynesboro. Within minutes of our arrival in masks of Richard Nixon and Bill Clinton, the local police appeared—summoned by residents who expected annual ghoulish pranks at the cemetery. The two officers—kids in their early twenties—didn't recognize Nixon, Clinton, or us. "I'm Jason Smith, the chief of staff to the President of the United States," I finally asserted. "This is the Secretary of HUD, and we're visiting the grave of President Jones. He's buried here. It's an important night."

"Why does the gravestone say 'Steve Albert'?"

"We gave him an alter ego."

"Who are you again?"

"Jason Smith, the president's chief of staff."

The cops faked a laugh at the Halloween high jinks by two semi-geezers and told us to move along before they charged us with trespass.

Leroy and I drove around while I generated the nerve for what came next. We returned to the cemetery through a back entrance, spent the night digging up Steven Albert, and finally stashed his casket in the back of Leroy's pickup. Leroy sped to the mall in front of the Capitol while I made signs. We unloaded the casket on the sidewalk.

Leroy disappeared with his truck before anyone recognized him. Having known all the crazies on the street, I exhibited a fair ability for creating a scene. I propped up the signs on the casket and exclaimed that I, Jason Ward Smith IV, had James Jefferson Jones's body right here on the sidewalk. At exactly 8 AM, in the middle of rush hour, before hundreds of commuters and congressional staffers involved in the impeachment hearings, I opened the casket. But to my astonishment, J3 wasn't there!

"Oh, fuck!" was the quote that made the newspapers and CNN. I looked pretty silly, but the U.S. had already written me off as a nut.

Now what?

A dozen police pounced on me and threw me in jail again. Carlos was still sitting in his cell and just said, "Welcome back, man. The chili still sucks. You got my new job yet?"

I played checkers and watched TV with Carlos for a week until the police hauled me into court where I met ace attorney Herb Schaklem, hired by Leroy. The judge, another good old boy appointed through J3, said, "Mr. Smith, you're charged with theft of a body in Waynesboro, Pennsylvania. It's a felony. You're going to be extradited." Needless to say, Herb didn't bail me out. I called Liz because I just knew she was behind my extended stay; but after picking up the phone, she disappeared.

I rode to Pennsylvania in the back seat of a cruiser and became the celebrity of the Waynesboro jail for two months. I wasn't allowed any visitors—not even Leroy or Sarah who wrote to tell me she was trying to help. I didn't see an attorney, either, although I learned quite a bit of law from Herb Schaklem's cousin Vidi, a blind and disbarred attorney sharing the jail with me.

Meanwhile, the image of J3, virtually alive as a hologram/robot/video, appeared all over the media. White House Television showed Robby-Bobby as a powerful VP preparing for the 2008 election. Finally, one morning I awoke to the news screaming throughout the jail: "PRESIDENT ASSASSINATED BY TERRORIST!" A suicide driver had rammed J3's convoy of SUVs headed for a fundraiser for the Forum of Former Fabricators. Jimmy Jeff Jones was blown into three large pieces—no doubt Jimmy, Jeff, and Jones. Some radical group claimed responsibility.

Beelzebob was sworn in as president and in his first speech promised to wipe out the killers of J3—including the associate of the suicide bomber, one Dr. Axel Hatchet. The nation mourned J3, just as Liz predicted it would. President Bobs gave a perfect eulogy at Arlington National Cemetery.

The local Waynesboro judge eventually let me out of jail after I convinced him that I had simply dug up a piece of wood—since nobody was in the casket. The judge winced at my explanation but concluded that you can't steal a body if there's no body. Besides, he agreed, Steven Albert didn't even exist. "It's a good spook story, though," he said.

I walked out of jail with enough money for bus fare; somewhere during my incarceration, I'd given up my cash for jello treats and hamburgers. Because Liz had tied up my savings and checking accounts, I knew I wouldn't get to them without a fight or a midnight raid on my buried money vault at Hickory Hill. I knew eventually I would recover Buster Keaton, my money, and visitation with my kids, but I didn't have the faintest idea how to enforce the promises without some mouthpiece like Herb Schaklem covering my back. Unfortunately, I didn't trust Herb very much. So I returned to Kansas Avenue.

When I ingloriously arrived in DC on a bus, I discovered from Leroy that President Fenster had fired all the cabinet officers except Paul. Paul saved his own ass by prosecuting Ron Durondon, George W. and Jeb Bush (for being Bushes), and former officials of the J3 Administration for corruption, obstruction of justice, fraud, and general hubris. Leroy fortunately had built up some savings, bought an apartment on Kansas Avenue, and ended up with his feet on the ground. He let me room with him until I could get myself back in an upright position. Although I had a place to stay, I found myself wandering the streets again—not actually without a home or without money but more or less without purpose.

These wanderings led to my becoming a *de facto* social worker. Every morning I showed up at the shelters, stuffed food in a van, and drove around DC looking for the wretched. When I couldn't find enough wretched, I worked on the miserable and the rotten. Sometimes I gave the food to tourists or stray dogs or ate it myself. I didn't bother to call Liz and demand anything. I missed Buster Keaton and my kids, but I didn't want them to see me so depressed and down and out. I asked Leroy not to tell anyone I was staying with him.

Then fate or God intervened again. One day as I stepped from behind some bushes after feeding Carlos, Big Tits, Amy, and Shark in Lafayette Park across from the White House, Sarah appeared out of nowhere looking goddess-like. She seemed as surprised as I was and said she'd been searching for me for months—had divorced Paul and wanted me to come with her. Her concern made me feel the old warmth. She smiled and hugged me—but then dragged me toward the White House.

"Where are you taking me?" I asked.

"The White House. Just shut up and don't say anything. Why haven't you called me?"

"I'm not the same person that worked in the White House."

She turned to me. "Well, you're more like the old you again—a homeless person. Kiss me."

"You want me to kiss you? I'm filthy. At least let me take a shower before I visit the White House."

"No time." But I kissed her.

We walked across the street to the White House. This time the guards let us in. In my awful, smelly clothes, I was directed to the new President of the United States, Robert "Beelzebob" Fenster.

"Smitty!" he greeted me in his raspy, glass-vibrating voice. "I like your wardrobe—ha ha ha—did you buy that in jail?"

"Very funny," I said.

"Welcome back. We missed you. We need honest, hard-working people in the new Fenster White House. Once you get cleaned up, I'm assigning you to our new chief of staff, Deuce Brucie. And Sarah is going to become my chief domestic adviser. I want you both to help me."

"Where's Liz?"

"She doesn't work here. She's home with your kids—Lincoln, Lucien, Laertiades, LeMonde, and Lyman—preparing them to become future presidents."

I looked around, thought about all of the fun I had, the power, the good life, a house, a wife, children, a dog, peace, democracy, and freedom. And then I thought about all the lies. I looked at Sarah.

"I love you both, but no thanks."

I turned and walked out—and, guess what? Sarah followed me.

Now, twelve years later in 2020, both Sarah and I live on Kansas Avenue in one of the huge apartment buildings I own—as do-gooders handing out food, finding rooms for mothers with young children, and watching out for homeless who need blankets and advice and clean needles. Carlos helps us—ever since I bought the April Showers Hotel and hired him as the entertainment director—but he prefers the outdoor life. Liz gave me $200 million in the divorce settlement, which I invested well and now use for the unchosen. She lets me visit L1 through L5, although they're teenagers and recite the "Gettysburg Address" daily to train for their role as leaders.

Buster Keaton came with me after I settled in, but died shortly afterward in his sleep—and I cried when I couldn't wake him. He was the most honest thing in my life.

Occasionally, politicians ask my advice, but I always tell them I don't know nuttin' but mutton—and I really don't know much. I do know that being perfect is a stupid illusion. And I do know that I didn't need the Wiz to give me a conscience.

The world did a strange thing after I left the White House. It erased the history of J3 like a hard drive on a computer—by writing over it. Instead of remembering J3 as president from 2001 to 2008, it portrayed George W. Bush as president. For a lot of money and immunity from prosecution for him and Jeb—who wanted to become the third Bush president—George W. went along with the worldwide revision of history. Soon people forgot everything about James Jefferson Jones—although some wondered why his name appeared so prominently at Arlington National Cemetery and why so many children in the U.S. had names that began with J. Historians made up things about George W.—such as a terrorist attack on September 11, 2001, two preemptive wars, torture, secret prisons, indefinite detention without trial, and secret wiretapping. As Lincoln or P. T. Barnum asserted, you *can* fool all of the people some of the time and some of the people all of the time. I once thought you could fool all of the people all of the time, but I was wrong. I still remember everything. I wasn't ever fooled by J3 or Bush or by my own lies. Neither were Sarah and Leroy.

Without J3's benevolent dictatorship—without his Wizard of Ozness—the world returned to wars and poverty. Beelzebob, like J3, worked hard to become a Perfect President. He tried to do the right things in office—especially in the starry eyes of his supporters—but people eventually perceived that he, too, could be a devil. I can only hope that my kids will do better as presidents, if they get their chance. After all, as Lincoln observed, no government ever provided for its own termination.

978-0-595-40609-8
0-595-40609-2